Beyond Destiny
(The Afterlife Series Book 3)
By Deb McEwan

Cover Design by Jessica Bell

The Story So Far

Thanks for choosing 'Beyond Destiny', book three in my Afterlife Series. If you haven't read the first two books ('Beyond Death' and 'Beyond Life') I recommend you read them before this one. Here's a reminder of the story so far.

Big Ed has coerced three teenage girls into accompanying him to a party with the offer of free food and booze. They're unaware they will be groomed to have sex with older men. Melanie smells a rat, changes her mind and leaves the car before it reaches its destination.

Claire Sylvester dies in a RTA the morning after the best night of her life, along with Ron, her taxi driver. Her twin brothers Tony and Jim know she's dead before being told.

An angel named Gabriella tell Claire and Ron there's a backlog of souls waiting to be processed due to a natural disaster on earth. They're kept at Cherussola until the Committee decide their future, but are allowed to visit their friends and family. Claire discovers that her fiancée had a one-night stand with her best friend, and that her parents' marriage is a sham. Her father has been living a double-life for many years and she has a half-sister called Melanie. She also discovers she can communicate with her brothers and that she has powers that many dead souls do not.

Ron discovers his wife had an affair with Ken, his former boss. Ken dies and goes to Hell. He is reincarnated in different forms and his soul is in constant fear and pain.

Claire's mother Marion and Ron's wife Val meet by chance and join a charity. At a get together Tony meets Val's daughter Libby; they become romantically involved.

Val is already in a delicate state due to her husband's death. She is mugged (by three humans and

iv

one evil soul) during a training course and Ron begs Claire to do everything in her power to bring the muggers to justice. They discover where the muggers live and hang out, then hatch a clever plan to catch the muggers, involving Claire's twin brothers and Jim's girlfriend Fiona.

Melanie's friends tell her about their ordeal so she informs the police. She is kidnapped by Big Ed and his accomplice Sandy. Claire helps her brothers to find and save Melanie, but Big Ed escapes along with Sandy. He loses his temper and kills Sandy.

Having observed Claire and Ron's work with the twins, the Committee inform Gabriella that Claire is to remain where she is for a while to help people, while the angels are busy dealing with the backlog. Ron has the choice of whether to remain with Claire, or to move on to eternity. Claire is sent back to Earth to visit her family and friends, not knowing whether Ron will be in Cherussola when she returns.

On her pleasant journey upwards Sandy feels a rough jolt. The Committee have decided that she was complicit in Big Ed's crimes so must go to Hell. The decision causes a disagreement and Gabriella's brother is removed from the Committee by his mother Amanda.

Sandy suffers torture, and humiliation in Hell but refuses to cooperate with the demons. They return her to Earth to suffer in many different guises. The Committee eventually relent and save her between reincarnations.

Unable to return to Cherussola, Claire spends time watching her family and friends. Tony and Libby marry in Gretna Green while their mothers are in Zambia, working in an orphanage for their charity. When Gabriella returns Claire to Cherussola, she introduces her to Sandy. Ron decides he wants to stay with Claire and look out for his wife Val, so delays his journey to heaven. Claire ensures that Libby knows her father watched her wedding.

Big Ed, now calling himself Gary, has fled the country and had cosmetic surgery to alter his looks. He is still supplying men with young girls but has a legitimate building business for cover. Marion and Val meet him while in Zambia. Val is instantly attracted to him but Marion has a bad feeling – the women fall out but Marion's instincts prove to be correct. Girls go missing from the orphanage, some presumed dead from animal attacks.

Claire meets the angel Raphael who is Gabriella's twin. The attraction is mutual.

Claire's father Graham overcomes his many problems and turns his life around by becoming a body-builder. His ex girlfriend Carol softens and they eventually get back together.

Claire has a near miss and is saved from Hell by Raphael, Gabriella and some others. Back home Gabriella explains that Claire is being recruited to help the fight against evil. She explains how some evils are contained in a hard to access cave known by the locals as Hell on Earth. A number of evil souls in the guise of cockroaches are watched over by angels, disguised as bats.

Jim and Fiona marry and Tony and Libby receive a blessing at the same time.

With help from the angels and spirits, Big Ed is eventually caught and jailed for his heinous crimes. He meets an untimely death in a foreign prison and is sent to Hell.

Claire, her angel lover Raphael and his mother try to avoid Hell's gates while fighting the demons. While they are preoccupied, serpents amass outside the cave know as Hell on Earth.

Chapter 1

Claire had no idea how long they'd been fighting the demons. She only knew they should have lost the battle ages ago. If she'd had time to think about it properly, she would have been worried, very worried...

*****

It was the second day Libby hadn't been able to contact her mother and she was concerned. Her mother-in-law Marion, who was also her mother's best friend, had called to say she hadn't spoken to Val for two days. They were worried and didn't bother with the niceties as they met outside Val's front door. There was no answer so Libby used her key. All the curtains were drawn and the air was stale. There were a few dishes in the sink but no sign of uneaten or half-eaten meals. After running around and quickly checking each room downstairs, they almost collided at the bottom of the stairs. Libby looked upwards to the closed bathroom door; instinctively she knew her mother was in there. Her heart hammered in her chest and she started shaking. Feeling light-headed she took the hand that her mother-in-law offered, then followed Marion towards the bathroom.

When Marion pushed open the door Libby gasped. Her hand flew involuntarily to her mouth to suppress a scream. Val lay unconscious next to the bath, surrounded by a pool of blood. Marion noticed that blood trickled from a wound in her friend's arm then realised thankfully, that Val was alive. She rushed to her, only then seeing the vodka bottle laying by her side and the lump on Val's head.'

'Phone an ambulance, Libby.' Libby was rooted to the spot, eyes agog like a Bush baby.

'Now!'

Her mother-in-law's voice spurred her into action so she did as instructed. When Marion lifted Val's arm her friend groaned and opened her eyes. It took a second for her to realise that Marion and Libby were with her and she struggled to sit up.

'It's okay, Val. Just relax. The ambulance is on its way.'

Later, when Val was settled in the hospital Libby leaned over and kissed her mother's forehead. It made her feel better.

'Dad's watching over you, Mum. You're going to be all right.'

Libby still missed her father and thought of him every day. He'd died when he crashed the taxi he was driving, and tragically so had Claire, his passenger. The deaths had united the families and as well as Marion and Val being best friends, Libby was married to Tony, one of Claire's twin brothers.

Libby returned to the present when she thought she saw a flicker of recognition on her mother's face, but wasn't sure if she'd imagined it. A herd of elephants could have stampeded through the hospital and her mother would still be sleeping such was the strength of the drugs that had been administered. She walked to the door then exited the room closing it quietly behind her. It made absolutely no difference to Val.

'How is she?' Marion had dark circles under her eyes and looked totally drained. Understandable really, thought Libby, after all her own mother had been through. Marion was a proper friend and she would be forever grateful for her support and intervention.

2

'We should have spotted the signs,' Libby looked away and into the distance. 'I should have noticed something.'

Marion knew she blamed herself. They both did. She should have known Val wasn't strong enough to cope and should have ignored her stubbornness, and protestations that she could handle it. Alarm bells should have rang when Val started to dress differently, covering up more than usual. Although she would get first-class care now and her physical wounds would heal, neither her daughter nor best friend were sure if she was mentally strong enough to make a full recovery.

Chapter 2 – Six Months Earlier

The ringing phone woke Val. She ignored it until it stopped then picked it up to check the time. Eleven o'clock. Val put the phone on silent, lay back down and closed her eyes. She spent the rest of the morning the same way she had the previous four days - wondering why she'd trusted Gary who's real name, she now knew, was Big Ed. Such was the monumental affect he'd had on her life, she knew he would always be Gary to her however hard she tried to think of him by his given name. She would have remained in bed but the constant hammering on the front door was jarring her nerves and she couldn't ignore it any longer.

Val opened the door just enough to see who was there.

'Can we come in please, Mum?'

'It's not really convenient.'

'We need to speak to you,' added Marion and Val reluctantly opened the door, standing aside for them to enter. Marion and Libby tried to hide their shock as they looked at the bedraggled woman in front of them wondering how they'd break the news. Val didn't seem interested as she sat on the blue leather armchair. Looking around, her visitors could see ripped sections of newspaper strewn around the lounge and trailing into the other rooms. Some had splashes of dark red on them and Libby could picture her mother, drunk and distraught, tearing the papers to shreds. A knowing look passed between the visitors.

'We'll have a bit of a tidy up then I'll make you a nice cup of tea, Mum.' Her mother ignored her so Libby and Marion quietly gathered the newspaper pieces then took them to the kitchen, hoping that Val couldn't see the articles about the child trafficker and his naive charity worker girlfriend. They needn't have bothered; the damage had already been done.

4

Libby filled the kettle then switched it on. 'We can't tell her, not when she's in this state,' she whispered so her mother wouldn't hear.

'We have to, Libby.' Marion held her daughter-in-law's arms. 'What if she sees it on the news or reads about it on the Internet. We can't risk her finding out that way.'

They made the drinks and returned to the lounge. Marion set Val's mug of tea down next to her and sat on the arm of her chair. 'I'm really sorry, Val, but we have bad news.'

Val looked at her friend and daughter. She'd been deceived and the man she both loved and hated was rotting in a foreign jail. Her name and picture was all over the papers and although most of the press had lost interest, people whispered everywhere she went. On top of all of this she'd been sacked from her charity worker job because association with her would cause irreparable harm to the organisation. And Marion and Libby had bad news! She looked at them and snorted but neither found any amusement in the situation.

Libby took a breath. 'Big Ed is dead, Mum. He was attacked in the prison and ...' her words trailed off.

'His name's Gary.'

Sitting on the arm of her mother's chair she put an arm around her. Val leaned into her daughter's body and cried, quietly at first. Eventually the sobs wracked her whole body. Marion found it hard to believe her friend could cry for the evil scumbag who had ruined so many lives. As well as murder, child trafficking and his attempt at seducing Val, he had kidnapped Melanie, her ex-husband's lovechild. Thankfully, Melanie had been rescued and Marion was inordinately proud of her twins who had helped put Big Ed behind bars. She tried not to think of the terrible way he'd died but hoped he was rotting in Hell, getting everything he deserved. Unfortunately, her hopes were in vain.

Both Marion and Libby offered to stay with Val but she insisted on being alone. 'Look, it was a shock but now I can draw a line under that part of my life and start over. It's not as if Gary was my soul mate or anything.'

They could see she was putting on a brave face but neither was convinced she was well enough to be left on her own. Marion looked at her watch, she would happily cancel her hair appointment if Val needed her.

'Why don't you come and stay with me?' Marion had recently moved to a new apartment nearer to Libby and Tony's home, so would be closer and more convenient for visits from Libby.

'You know you're always welcome to stay with us, Mum.'

'I'm fine, really I am,' Val smiled kindly. 'I just need to be on my own for a while, now come on, shoo. I'll speak to you both tomorrow.' It was a different Val that chivvied them to the front door and they hugged and said goodbye. Knowing her as they did, they should have spotted the warning signs. Each would spend many sleepless nights in future wondering why they chose to ignore them.

Val closed the door and leaned against it, the smile had disappeared. Her shoulders sagged as she walked to the kitchen and opened the cupboard under the sink. She leaned into the back and removed the vodka bottle that was hidden behind the bleach and other cleaning products. Placing the vodka on the worktop she took three knives out of the knife block and chose the sharpest. With the knife and the vodka in hand she slowly climbed the stairs. Putting the vodka and knife in the bathroom Val went to her bedroom and switched on the iPod. She turned up the volume on

Lana Del Ray's *Born to Die*, removed her top and returned to the bathroom. The first cut was easy after a swig of vodka. Val experienced such a sense of relief when she felt the pain and saw the blood dripping from the wound in her arm. For the first time in ages she was in control and able to blank out everything that had happened since she'd met Gary. She felt good.

Chapter 3

Gabriella flapped her wings and frowned in concentration. Having guided Claire since her arrival in Cherussola, she never imagined she would be contemplating her rescue from Hell's dark doors. Or that of her own brother and mother. They'd been fighting to capture Big Ed, but Raphael had been overpowered by evils. She couldn't decide whether Claire's actions had been incredibly brave or stupid when she'd followed her lover. Amanda, Gabriella and Raphael's mother, had decided she was going to save them both. The angels Gabriella had sent on a rescue mission hadn't returned and now she was worried. She missed the wise counsel of her mother and brother and didn't want to appear indecisive by asking for advice from God and the Committee. After mulling it over, she decided to mount her own rescue. Hell would break loose if the three were captured, along with the angel Zach who Satan had taken ages ago, and she used this as an excuse for her actions. Gabriella's emotional involvement made her lose impartiality and she gathered the hosts, made a rousing speech and gave her orders. Buoyed up, they followed where she led, ready to tackle the harbingers of evil and determined to win the battle, if not the war.

Had she known the ramifications of her decision Gabriella would have been shocked to the core; it would be some time before the full consequences became apparent.

*****

A number of demons disguised as snakes were outside the cave known locally as *infierno terrenal*, the English translation was *Hell on Earth*. They knew they were sacrificial lambs but were also aware that if they refused to carry out this particular duty, the pain and consequences would be much worse. Nothing happened when the few devoured the bats as they left the dark cave when the sun went down. They summoned more slithering demons and they all gorged themselves on the bats. Still nothing arrived to end the activity of the snakes. The demons felt a shift in the atmosphere and took immediate advantage. They realised this could be the opportunity they had waited for as long as any of them could remember. More and more snakes arrived to devour the bats, hoping to pass incredible news to their leaders, and also hoping for relief from further torment and torture into the bargain.

The large number of good souls ascending alerted the Committee that something was wrong. Checks were carried out and it was quickly determined there hadn't been a full-scale disaster on Earth. As the first old souls started to arrive the guardians summoned them to the gates of the Committee Chambers. There was disbelief when the truth was passed to the Committee. The cave had been breached. The majority of the bats were dispatched to Cherussola and heaven in traumatic and painful ways, and the evil souls that had been contained in the cave in the guise of cockroaches, were now loose. The cleverest amongst them would be wreaking havoc in no time. Those that were not so clever would be delivered to Hell in order to receive new direction and orders from their evil leaders.

The Committee realised they'd been found napping and hadn't provided adequate direction for some of their new angels and souls. God called for an explanation from Gabriella. He heard about her mission shortly after and demanded to speak to her if or when she returned. The Committee discussed how to deal with the havoc that would surely erupt on Earth in the near future.

9

God was not at all confident of a quick and satisfactory resolution.

*****

On her way to the rescue Gabriella found a number of lost souls. She detailed a few angels to look after them, not wanting to deplete her fighting force by too many. They carried on their way and the closer they got the more skirmishes they had to deal with. She was surprised the evils weren't as organised as expected. It was as if some were missing and she wondered what they could be up to. One of her number pointed to a shape in the distance and Gabriella tried to shake off her feeling of foreboding as she concentrated on the individual. She noticed the wings and her mind worked overtime as the outline started to come into focus as the angel neared. Too big to be female, his head was down and he was moving with some speed but out of control. It wasn't her mother, Raphael or Claire so it could only be...

'Zach! Zach!' he didn't hear and was spinning out of control as he neared. She ordered a number of angels to quickly form five rows behind her and told them to tense for a substantial impact. Gabriella had just enough time to flex her wings before putting herself in the way of Zach's trajectory. He careered into her and she enveloped him, the momentum of the impact driving them quickly backwards into the other angels. They eventually slowed down and came to a stop. Gabriella tried to wake him to no avail. He was battered and bruised and there was a nasty deep cut in his throat. His essence was weakening and she knew if they didn't get him back quickly and give him time to heal, he might not make it. Even if he did rest he still might not pull through but she had to ensure he had a chance. For the second time her thoughts were interrupted as she looked below her.

10

'Something's changed!' Claire had the time and energy to shout and knew the enemy was getting weaker. She felt the first stirrings of hope within her soul and tried to suppress the feeling while concentrating on the current wave of demons. They didn't seem as strong or sadistic as others she'd fought and she felt the light of optimism taking hold. She couldn't see Raphael or Amanda but hoped they might be able to hear or sense her presence. Somebody did sense her presence. She was amazed to hear a familiar whoosh, and to see Gabriella appear in front of her with angels around her as far as the eye could see. The hosts were engaged in battles but Gabriella was surrounded by a circle that no demon had the strength to break. She was holding an angel that Claire could only describe as broken.

'Where's my mother and Raphael?' asked Gabriella and Claire noticed she hadn't needed to shout to be heard.

'We were separated by the sheer force of the enemy,' Claire shuddered. 'I don't know how long I've been fighting on my own and I don't know if they're lost for good.' She wouldn't allow herself time to think the worst as this would result in loss of concentration and in all likelihood give the demons further opportunity to take her to Hell.

Gabriella could see that Claire was mentally strong but was at her limit, physically. She was determined to find her mother and brother and knew that in her present state, Claire would be more of a hindrance than help. She quickly called for two of her lieutenants and issued orders. They waited while she explained to Claire. 'You'll be safe as long as you do exactly as I say. Any deviation will result in capture. Do you understand?'

Claire nodded but Gabriella knew how stubborn and single-minded she could be.

'This is the only chance I have of rescuing my mother and Raphael. If I have to worry about you or come to your rescue they could suffer for it.' Gabriella was satisfied with the effect her words had on Claire. If there was a chance Claire could be reunited with Raphael, she would do exactly as told. Gabriella banked on it. Claire joined her angel guards and two others who were now holding the broken angel. As they formed a circle of love she centred herself and pushed aside any non-loving thoughts and memories. They ascended slowly and she wasn't sure how much later they arrived in Cherussola, safe and sound. She had never been so pleased to feel the comfort of the cream leather sofa. As she sank into its unfathomable depths she knew she was home and for the first time in ages Claire wasn't frightened. Though totally drained and still in shock from the months of battling pure evil, she was still surprised they hadn't encountered any demons or evils on their return journey. When she regained her senses she would give herself time to think about it, there was something niggling at her but she was tired, so very tired.

*****

As Harry's current cockroach body took its last breath, he waited for his next cockroach reincarnation to begin and screamed at the injustices his soul had to bear. When he next opened his eyes he immediately felt the changes and his screams turned to whoops of delight. He examined his teenage boy persona then waited as if it were a trick. Reality eventually sunk in and he knew that for a while anyway, he wasn't going to be a cockroach. After he'd floated around for a bit getting used to his freedom from the dark cave and enjoying the feel of his old self, his euphoria changed to anger and thoughts of revenge. He wasn't strong enough to cause pain and grief to those who deserved it and knew he needed help. More determined than he'd been in his living years, Harry had a mission and the first part was to find and rescue his son, so they could avenge the injustices against them both.

*****

The ugly little dog looked at the woman as she chuntered on in her high-pitched voice. The dog couldn't stand the sound any more and she snapped and barked at her.

'Naughty, naughty girl,' she tapped the dog playfully and gave her a sloppy kiss, totally oblivious to the animal's anger and frustration. The *I'm a Barbie Girl* tune rang out and the owner placed the dog on the pavement, instructing it to be a good girl, while she rummaged in her designer bag for her phone.

The kids were squabbling in the back of the Land Rover Discovery and Penelope was already running late. She tried to ignore them while thinking about her *to do* list. After she dropped them off she had to go through the dinner party arrangements with her housekeeper, collect Barnaby's suit from the dry cleaners and somehow fit in the meeting with Barnaby's sister about her charity auction. Life was impossibly busy and she intended to speak to her husband regarding a suitable boarding school for the children. Penelope turned to berate them.

'For goodness sake, Octavia, do pipe down and, Tarquin, stop tormenting your sister.' Distracted, she didn't notice the angry fur-ball that ran out in front of her.

The owner screeched in horror as her beloved pet was squashed under the Discovery's wheel and Big Ed watched the two distressed women as his soul left the dog's body and floated in the atmosphere for a few seconds before being claimed. He felt the somehow familiar gnarled hands and for reasons he couldn't fathom, expected them to be replaced by soft ones. The

13

hands didn't change and the journey continued downwards until the evil soul was at last delivered to its spiritual home.

Chapter 4 – The Present

The school for people with special abilities, or SAPs as it was known to the staff, was located in a beautiful Scottish valley surrounded by rolling rugged hills and countryside. There were no other buildings in the area, the nearest village being some miles away. The school housed an eclectic mix of students along with the permanent staff. There were two wings. *A Wing* comprised of talented individuals who were recruited from the public, plus members of the military. They were trained as undercover agents in the fight against enemies or potential enemies of the State, and the most dangerous criminal elements of society. Some of the students in *B Wing* were also trained as undercover agents. In addition these students were recruited for their more unusual talents, which included claims of telepathy, magic, witchcraft and communication with the dead. Tests were on going to validate these claims but had so far proved inconclusive. All students had signed the Official Secrets Act and had enhanced government security clearance. Trust was an issue with many of the students in *B Wing* due to the unusual nature of their assertions. Though open-minded, the permanent staff were told to be sceptical until provided with concrete proof. The school perimeter was surrounded by barbed wire and employed armed guards. Visits from curious members of the public were few and far between. Successive governments had informed the public that the location was a high security facility and treatment centre for the most dangerous criminally insane members of society. The myth was validated by occasional news bulletins when infamous serial killers had been caught and the public informed they would be housed there. The crimes of some of these people had been so horrendous that not even the most curious members of the public would risk trying to get inside the facility, even if they were able to get past the armed guards who were all highly trained military or ex-military personnel. Due to media coverage of Big Ed's capture and subsequent demise and a little bit of digging, the Sylvester twins names had been brought to the attention of the SAP talent scout, and she started her campaign to recruit them to the cause.

On Thursday night Libby was with her mother. Fiona was playing netball and the twins were in their local having their weekly catch-up before the match started.

'So she's playing netball? Thought that was for schoolgirls.'

Jim laughed at Tony's comment. 'Don't let Fiona hear you say that. She says she's one of the youngest in her team and she's addicted to it already. Match nights are Thursday so that's handy.' They clinked glasses and Tony finished his pint then tapped the empty glass on the table while looking at his brother.

'Hint taken.' Jim finished his own drink and made his way to the bar. He looked around as the barman served other customers. About to give his own order he hesitated, noticing the middle-aged woman towards the end of the bar waiting patiently. He remembered his mother telling him and Tony that when women reach a certain age they become invisible. The world ignores them and turns its attention to those younger and perkier. According to their mother this meant having to queue longer at bars, to get tables in restaurants, having doors held open for them and all manner of other things that Jim had lost count of. The match was about to start and he didn't know why he chose this moment to be chivalrous, perhaps it was because of his mother.

'The lady was before me,' he nodded his head in her direction and she smiled gratefully at him as the barman took her order. Although dressed in forgettable clothing, Jim felt she had a certain air about her but put any further thoughts of this out of his mind as he placed his own order, paid for the two pints and hurried back to his seat.

Violet Hennessey returned to her corner booth where she could observe the twins while pretending to read her Kindle. As Tony approached the bar at half time she intercepted him and introduced herself.

'I'm Violet Hennessey and I work for the government. We're interested in training you and your brother for special projects.'

Tony was taken aback, but curious. 'What department and what projects?'

'I can't say any more in here,' she looked around noticing that Jim was watching them. 'Here's my card. Call me if you want to know more.'

Tony took the card and by the time he'd read the name and telephone number, the woman had disappeared.

'What was all that about?' asked Jim when Tony returned with the drinks.

'It was obviously some sort of wind up.' Tony relayed the conversation to his brother.

'What do you want to do?'

'Ignore it,' said Tony, 'and watch the rest of the match.' They chinked glasses again and turned to the screen but both were wondering about Violet Hennessey's words and the game was spoilt.

Outside the pub Violet smiled to herself. He would call. Curiosity always got the better of them.

*****

Harry's first meeting with his son wasn't what he'd hoped. Big Ed had initially blamed him for the way his earthly life had turned out and Harry had been surprised when he had attacked him, both physically and verbally. Big Ed hadn't been in the spirit world long enough to reach his full strength and was overcome by Harry, but not by much.

'Son, let's put the past behind us and work together. I'll be back after your initiation. Be strong.' He disappeared and so began the round of humiliation and torture that was Big Ed's welcome to Hell. His human death had been violent and painful. His subsequent lives were in the guise of female lap dogs so Big Ed knew all about humiliation. When the torture became unbearable he thought about revenge and his anger gave him strength. He endured the pain and deprivation and his masters soon recognised one of their own. The cleverer amongst them knew it was only a matter of time before the tables turned and the tortured would become the torturer. The initiation ended and some of the demons attempted to worm their way into Big Ed's good books by favouring him over others, and treating him as a superior. It didn't work. As soon as he was strong enough he sought out those who'd committed the vile acts against him and repaid them ten times over. His strength increased on an almost daily basis. He had no idea how long he'd been in Hell but decided it was time to seek out his father – knowing he could trust him to carry out his wishes – and repay some of the people who'd caused his suffering on Earth.

*****

By day three Violet was beginning to wonder whether one of the twins would actually call. Two days was the longest she'd ever had to wait and was grudgingly impressed they'd been able to hold off for so long. Her boss – who also happened to be her husband - had asked for an update and she'd told him all was in hand and he shouldn't concern himself. She would

18

definitely recruit the twins by the end of the week. It was day four after the conversation in the pub and as the seeds of doubt started to multiply in Violet's mind, her phone rang. She smiled when she saw the number.

'Hello, Tony.'

'How did you know it was me?'

'Never mind that for now, shall we meet on Thursday night? I know a quiet restaurant where we can talk in private.'

Tony followed the instructions and relayed them to his brother after hanging up.

On the Thursday evening Libby was preoccupied with her mother's condition and didn't notice Tony was lying when he told her he was going to the pub as usual, to watch the match with Jim. Jim and Fiona were saying goodbye in their home.

'Where you off tonight?' asked Fiona, noticing her husband wasn't dressed in his usual football top.

'Same as usual, Fi. Down the pub to watch the match.'

'Where's your football top?'

'What is this, fifty questions? I fancied wearing something different all right. It's not a crime is it?'

'Okay, okay, I only asked.'

They kissed goodbye and went their separate ways. Jim wondering if he'd overreacted and Fiona why her husband had been so defensive.

The restaurant was off a side road and the twins were shown to a secluded table where Violet Hennessey was already seated. She put down her Kindle and held out her hand to shake. After the formal introductions a waiter arrived and took their drinks order; beer for the men, bottles not pints, and dry white wine for Violet.

'I love this restaurant,' Violet opened her menu and glanced at it before looking at the twins. 'We use it often and the staff are our employees.'

19

'And who might *our* be?' asked Jim.

'Plenty of time for that later,' she smiled. Her unhurried attitude was beginning to annoy Jim.

'Look, let's cut to the chase. Who are you and what do you want?'

'Strapping lads like you must have big appetites. I recommend the steak, always cooked to perfection.'

Seeing his brother was about to lose it Tony gave him a warning look. 'Much as the food looks great, Violet, we're not going to stay here any longer unless you tell us what all this is about.'

She closed the menu and stopped any further pretence at small talk. 'You will already know the government has various agencies that carry out undercover operations. Yes?' The men nodded.

'Well I'm a representative from one of the more unusual training establishments and we want you to come and work for us.'

'To do what?' Jim asked the question but they were both intrigued.

'It will be undercover work, but first we need to find out whether you're suitable. Are you interested?'

'How can we say whether we're interested if we don't know what it entails?'

Tony asked and Violet noticed how the twins played word tag without even realising it.

'The school, because that's what it technically is, will train you in all aspects of undercover work and you'll be taught how to use your special talents to their utmost...'

'To what end?' interrupted Jim.

'As I was saying,' Violet silenced the twins with a look and Jim felt as he did when told off by his mother. 'Once your talents are developed you will be employed on special projects, an example of which is to help us catch the more elusive criminal elements of society.'

'You want to recruit us as spies?' Tony asked more to himself than anyone else and Jim was thinking the same.

Violet told them the suitability tests would take place in the South East and possibly elsewhere. If they agreed, they'd be away for a week. 'You understand that you can't discuss this with anyone and you will be required to sign the Official Secrets Act?'

Nonplussed by the conversation so far, they nodded in unison. The food arrived and the twins felt as if they were in a movie or dream, such was the impact of Violet's words. She changed the subject and brought the conversation around to family, friends and hobbies. The twins had told Violet everything she wanted to know, and she'd divulged little about herself in return.

After the waiter cleared away the main course Violet returned to the topic. 'I know you're between jobs, Jim and that yours doesn't really stretch you, Tony.'

They didn't bother to ask how she knew.

'So this could be an opportunity to stretch yourselves to your limits, provide a very much needed service to the public and keep our country safe.' She called for the bill without asking if they wanted anything further to eat or drink.

'Phone me tomorrow and let me know your answer. And whatever it is, remember that you can never discuss this conversation with anyone. Even your nearest and dearest.'

After their part in the capture of Big Ed the twins had become dissatisfied with their careers and had discussed their feelings with their wives, who in turn talked to their closest friends. Unbeknown to them this information had eventually found its way to Violet.

They nodded. After Violet paid the bill she stood up to leave and the twins stood. They shook hands and she left the restaurant. They were lost in their own thoughts and after a few seconds Tony spoke. 'Come on, let's get out of here.' Both already knew what their decision would be. The meeting with the enigmatic Violet Hennessey would change their lives forever.

Chapter 5

Melanie was in her bedroom working hard on her homework. Academic but practical too, she knew she was luckier than most and was determined to get good results in her 'A' levels.

Something didn't feel right and Mel felt the hairs on the back of her neck stand up. She looked up from her desk and shook her head, knowing full well that nobody else was in the room. Still, she couldn't shake off the weird feeling and she'd now lost concentration. Getting up she did a lazy cat-like stretch. Perhaps it was time to take a break. Mel turned on the TV then lay on her back on the bed. The noise was coming from the screen but she wasn't really listening. Trying to relax she still had an eerie feeling as if she was being watched.

The big black spider was of the chunky body variety with legs in proportion to the rest of it. It eyed up its victim from the edge of the bed as it moved along the quilt towards her. Not an ordinary spider it didn't scuttle along, but moved intelligently and stealthily with determination, so that Mel couldn't see it in her peripheral vision. It remembered what happened when it had been a human and intended to inflict maximum damage on the girl that it had kidnapped. The girl who had subsequently been rescued before he could sell her to the highest bidder.

Something was definitely giving Mel the creeps and she desperately felt the need for company. As she swung her legs over the side of the bed and put her hands next to her body, she felt an excruciating pain. It was as if someone had thrust a sharp needle into her palm and Mel felt the pain moving up her arm.

There was a knock at the front door. Mel's mother, Carol was surprised to see Marion when she opened it.

'Oh, Marion. What can I do for you?'

Ask me in for a start thought Marion, but Carol didn't, so still standing on the doorstep she asked if all was well with Melanie.

'She's fine. Why? Is something the matter?'

Carol grudgingly opened the door and indicated with her arm for Marion to come in.

'I'm really sorry to bother you but I had a dream last night that Mel...'

A terrifying scream came from Mel's bedroom and the women shared a quick glance before sprinting up the stairs, like the doors had opened at Harrods on the first day of the sales.

Mel had had the presence of mind to knock the spider off the bed with her uninjured hand and was holding her bitten arm at the elbow with the other hand, simultaneously jumping on the spider that had caused her injury.

That didn't go quite to plan, thought Big Ed as his soul floated away from what was left of the spider body. The gruesome, gnarled hands pulled him back down into the depths of Hell.

*****

Fiona wondered what was going on with Jim. He'd told her he needed a break and that Tony was paying for them to go on a hiking trip. It seemed unusual that Tony would go away while Libby was so stressed due to her mother's condition. She decided to give her sister-in-law a call. The answerphone kicked in on the landline so Fiona tried her mobile.

24

Libby started talking before Fiona had a chance to say hello. 'Hi, Fi you've saved me a job, I was going to call you later.'

She explained she was going to stay with Marion for a while. It was nearer the hospital and when Val was discharged she would join them so that Marion and Libby could look after her in shifts. 'I've told Tony to have his break while Mum's in hospital. He's not happy in work and he's talking about re-training. I can't think about that at the moment so I'm hoping Jim will help him sort it out.'

They chatted about life in general and arranged to meet later in the week. Fiona hung-up and felt better for her chat with Libby. She chuckled to herself wondering what Jim and Tony would conjure up on their hiking trip, fully expecting her husband to return with his head full of new career plans, which would undoubtedly involve Tony.

*****

Ron and Sandy found Claire on the couch in Cherussola. As the realisation of what she'd experienced started to sink in, Claire started shaking and Sandy watched while Ron held her until she stopped. Now totally overwhelmed by exhaustion, Claire couldn't stay awake. Ron felt her leaving before he had a chance to explain what had happened on Earth and to tell her how worried he was about Val. At least he could stop worrying about Claire now. She would need all her energy to fight the demons that had been let loose and he wondered if even with Claire's special talents, the likes of Big Ed and his evil associates could ever be defeated.

*****

The pain was excruciating and every time Raphael thought he was going to pass out, the demons stopped and he was brought back from the edge of consciousness. He had no idea how long he'd been suffering but was desperate for it to end. This time it felt as if his eyes were on fire and he couldn't see a thing. Occasionally one of them would poke another part of his body. It was a supreme effort but he took his mind off the pain for a moment. Something wasn't quite right. Instead of the usual organised torture the current round was beginning to feel random. The painful prods seemed tentative rather than determined. Forcing himself to pay attention Raphael could hear the demons shouting at each other and arguing. He guessed these were mostly minor evils who plainly lacked direction and leadership. The pain in his eyes gradually lessened and he was eventually able to see. There were fires everywhere and a collection of evils gathered around each one. Raphael could just see his mother and she nodded at him. In the distance he could see another collection of evils tormenting two good souls who must have been despatched to the wrong place, for reasons unknown. The fog in his mind started to clear and whilst he was relieved the torture had lessened, he knew all was not well. The senior evils must have had a very good reason for leaving their subordinates in charge of two high grade angels, who they must know would eventually escape their clutches. With the hope came clarity and Raphael knew this was their best chance. Clearly his mother was thinking the same. As she looked toward him he could feel her instructions enter his thoughts. They were leaving and it was their duty to rescue the misplaced good souls and take them with them. She would fight their tormentors and she wanted him to rescue the others. They would then form a circle and make good their escape. His mother made it sound so straightforward and simple but Raphael knew they'd have to endure further suffering. He composed himself and took his lead from her. As soon as she made a move, her son jumped into action.

26

His earlier assumptions were correct, as the majority of demons left behind were really low grade. Unfortunately for Raphael as soon as he made a move he was ambushed by the strongest who attached themselves to his side and leg, biting and cutting. As he managed to detach one another soon took its place, intent on slowing his progress and causing maximum pain before his escape. While he tried to deal with these his mother was able to swat the others away as if they were merely irritating flies, but there were too many for her to come to his aid. There was a sudden whoosh and Gabriella appeared by Raphael's side. They didn't speak as she helped him remove and defeat the clinging demons. When they'd succeeded they quickly rescued the two bewildered souls and Gabriella told Raphael that Claire and Zach had already been saved. She explained that her hosts had dealt with many evils but they'd expected more as they neared Hell. The angels should have been relieved as they ascended in their circle; instead they were concerned. The good souls they'd liberated were shockingly quiet. They didn't have a clue where they were, who they were with, or what was happening. Amanda, Gabriella and Raphael did their best to concentrate on their journey, unwilling to face the fact that while they were away, the worst must have happened on Earth.

Chapter 6

The Land Cruiser was already in the car park around the corner from the restaurant when the twins arrived. The driver saw their approach in his rear view mirror and jumped out of the car. Tony's first impression was that the middle-aged man looked average and forgettable. He didn't yet realise that it took some effort for the SAPs operatives to perfect this look. He introduced himself as Dave, handed his mobile phone to Jim and indicated that he should answer when it rang. Violet Hennessey said hello and gave Jim a password he was to confirm with Dave. When the conversation ended Dave gave the correct word and Jim told Tony they could proceed with the journey. They hadn't yet been told where they were going but Dave now explained they were on their way to a military establishment in Aldershot, *The Home of the British Army*, and would be tested for suitability.

'What sort of tests?' asked Tony.

'Don't know.'

'Have you been through these tests?'

'Look, guys you'll find out everything you need to know when we get there and meet the others. Until then sit back and enjoy the ride.'

They hadn't been told anyone else would be there but knew there was no point in asking whom the others were. Dave saw the look pass between the twins and was satisfied he wouldn't have to answer any further questions.

The journey passed quickly. When they arrived at the barracks the gate guard lifted the barrier without checking Dave's ID. He drove through the camp until they came to a building that stood alone, some distance away from the others.

Dave turned off the engine and faced the twins. 'This is it guys, we're here. Grab your bags and follow me.'

They entered a reception area where a female soldier was working on a computer.

'Good morning gentlemen. Please stand in front of the camera,' she nodded at the camera protruding from a wall, 'one at a time please.' Less than a minute later they were handed their photo IDs and told to keep them with them at all times during their stay. 'Please take a seat and Ryan will be along shortly to start your induction.'

Both thought Ryan was probably a soldier although he was dressed in civilian clothes. Tall and ruggedly handsome he looked like a rugby player and neither brother would like to get into a tangle with this man. Despite flicking her hair, smiling beautifully and following his every move with her come to bed eyes, Ryan appeared not to notice the soldier receptionist, and Tony rightly assumed the big man wasn't short of female attention. Following the introductions Ryan led them down a dark, empty corridor and opened a door. There were four other people in the room. The twins were surprised to see a geeky looking man who was either a teenager or in his early twenties, an obese man of indeterminate age and an older man and woman who looked like a couple. As if reading their minds Ryan introduced them to the others and explained they would all undergo written suitability tests. They would then go their different ways and undertake further tests depending on their individual talents. The twins took a seat and switched on their computers. Questions and images appeared on the screen and all six were soon immersed in the information on their own monitors, ignoring the others. Following completion they were escorted from the room and returned to the reception area. Tea, coffee and biscuits arrived and they took a break, chatting amongst themselves for a while. The twins rightly assumed that the others had been given the same instructions as they, as nobody divulged any personal details. More people arrived in plain clothes and spoke to the other candidates who disappeared with the officials shortly after. Ryan returned to the reception area dressed in combat trousers, boots and a t-shirt.

'Guys, go and change into your boots and fatigues and we'll start the physical tests. You'll need the rucksacks from your lockers and the kit that's in them. I'll explain more when you're ready.'

Violet Hennessey had given them a list of items to bring and told them they would undergo extensive mental and physical tests. Neither twin had found the earlier test difficult and as they considered themselves to be fit, hoped to find the physical tests a doddle.

The female soldier gave them their locker keys and directions to the changing facilities and although confident in their own abilities, they didn't know what to expect so were beginning to feel apprehensive.

Shortly after and dressed for outdoors, they met Ryan in reception.

'Hope you like hills and rain?'

The twins didn't like the sound of this.

'We're off to Brecon,' he smiled, 'and the next few days, my friends, will either make or break you.'

*****

Carol paled when she saw Melanie's wound. It looked as if it was spreading to the rest of her hand and arm. Having dealt with bite injuries during her volunteer stint in Africa, Marion immediately took charge. Although first aid trained she realised this was beyond her expertise and called an ambulance. She'd been given advice on what action to take and while they were waiting she told Mel to remain standing, then quietly informed Carol they had to keep her as still and as calm as possible in order to slow the spread of the poison. She applied a bandage as she'd been instructed and this did help to slow the progression of the poison. The ambulance took Mel, her mother and Marion to Guys Hospital where they held a number of antivenins. The specialised staff awaited Mel's arrival and the doctor fired questions at them straight away.

'What sort of snake was it?'

'It was a spider,' answered Carol. 'A bloody big one.' The mess on the carpet in Mel's room had been big enough for Carol to notice even though Mel had been harmed. Mr Stevens hadn't seen anything like this before and he disappeared to make a hasty call to the National Reptile and Arachnid Research Centre. A few minutes later he returned with the suggested antivenin and it was quickly administered to Mel. As soon as the antivenin entered her bloodstream it started to help her immune system fight the spider poison and halted the spread of the wound. Mr Stevens said that Mel was to remain in hospital for her condition to be monitored, but he was confident they had treated her in time to prevent any long-term damage. Carol was worried but relieved that due to Marion's quick thinking, Mel's wound was not life-threatening. Any negative thoughts about her rival for Graham's attention left Carol and she finally realised she didn't have to dislike Marion any more.

'I can't thank you enough, Marion.' Tears ran slowly down Carol's cheeks.

Marion knew how distressing it was to see your children suffer and she responded by putting her arms around Carol and hugging her. Big Ed would have been irritated to discover that his attempt at killing Mel had actually healed a rift between her mother and Marion, whom he despised.

When Carol looked in on Mel she was sleeping. Marion suggested it would be a good time for them to go and get some of Mel's personal items so she would feel more comfortable when she awoke. As they left Carol remembered that Marion's visit had been unscheduled.

'When I answered the door this morning, you asked if Mel was all right and now this.' Carol raised her eyebrows.

'Ah, right.' Marion gathered her thoughts wondering if Carol would think her crazy. 'This is going to sound really weird but I can only tell it as it is.'

'Go on.'

'I've had a few dreams in the past that something's going to happen, and the dreams have come true.'

Carol didn't say a word and Marion took that as a signal to continue.

'When I was working in Africa I dreamt that my son and Val's daughter married without telling us. It wasn't until we arrived home that we discovered they had.'

Carol thought for a moment. 'But if they were seeing each other anyway, surely that might have been wishful thinking or your subconscious taking things a bit further.'

'But they'd only been together for five minutes!' Carol looked dubious but Marion had started so felt compelled to tell her about Mel. 'Last night I dreamt Mel had been bitten and I heard her screaming in my dream. I tried to shake it off this morning but couldn't... and you know the rest.'

'Was she in her bedroom in your dream?'

'I can't remember where she was, only that I heard her say ouch in surprise and then the screaming. But the screaming was the same as we both heard, Carol,' Carol frowned. 'Look, I'm sorry if this is upsetting for you but I can only tell you the truth.'

'I don't know what to think to be honest, Marion. The main thing is that thanks to you, Mel's going to be okay,' the frown turned to a smile. 'Whether the dream was a coincidence or you being able to see into the future doesn't really matter. Thank you.'

'My pleasure.'

'Saying that,' said Carol, 'I'd be a bit worried if I were you, especially if you don't know which dreams are going to come true and which ones aren't?'

Marion already had this concern and wondered why this was happening to her.

*****

Big Ed didn't want to be a spider or any other effing insect or animal for that matter. In Hell he was strong and formidable and feared by all, other than the very senior and most evil masters. However, he hadn't yet been able to build up enough strength to be a serious contender on Earth and this he found very frustrating. He was even more irritated that he had to rely on his useless father to teach him how to harness the limited strength he did have, and to put it to best use. It was in this frame of mind that Harry found him on the current visit to Earth, and he hoped to improve his son's mood by the surprise visit they were about to make.

Back at her own place Marion put the kettle on and stared out of the kitchen window. So, Val would leave hospital within the next few days but now Melanie was in hospital too, poor kid. She tried to make sense of the dream and the situation but couldn't fathom it all. She'd have a cup of tea - that always made her feel better. Then she'd sort out the bills she would have done earlier had she not been compelled to check on Melanie. Marion turned around and expected

33

to see someone in the room, such was the intense feeling she was not alone.

'Who is it?'

There was nobody there but she wasn't convinced. She checked upstairs and down and she was definitely alone. How weird because she couldn't shake off the feeling of being watched. It wasn't a pleasant experience. Marion re-boiled the kettle, poured her tea then opened the drawer to get some paperclips. She harrumphed when she saw they were all inter-twined. As she impatiently tried to separate the clips Marion asked herself why, when they were stored as single clips, they somehow linked together when next needed.

Harry giggled to himself as he watched Marion become frustrated with the paperclips. He nodded to his son who entered the drawer containing the bills. Big Ed moved two envelopes so they fell down the back of the drawer out of sight.

Marion still couldn't shake off the feeling of being watched but tutted, telling herself to get a grip. As she opened the drawer to remove the paperwork she wondered if her dream about Melanie and the fact it had come true had spooked her. Sorting through the envelopes on the table she couldn't find the ones she needed. She frowned thinking this strange, as she'd definitely put them in there the week before. Or had she? With everything going on with Val and now Melanie she might have been distracted. Marion began to doubt herself and looked in all the other places she might have stored the envelopes. When she still couldn't find them she returned to the cabinet and lifted the drawer completely out, placing it on the floor. She went through every item becoming more and more frustrated as she did so. Finding nothing she removed the other drawers checking all their contents to no avail. Some time later Marion found the envelopes at the bottom of the cabinet, stuck right at the back. She intended to pay them on line and went to switch on the computer.

'Bloody great!' she said out loud when nothing happened. 'Something funny's going on.' Marion plugged in the computer and looked around. She never removed the plug. I must have a poltergeist she thought to herself and laughed out loud. Her laughing stopped as she wondered about what had happened and if there really was a strange presence in the house. Shaking her head again she berated herself and turned on the computer. As she did so she remembered the washing machine had completed its cycle and Marion decided to put the washing in the tumble dryer as the computer went through its start up.

'Jesus H Christ!' she shouted when she couldn't find two socks. Now in a foul mood she returned to the computer and went about her business, ignoring the sounds from upstairs. Everything happened at once and her day got even worse when Marion convinced herself that the noisy central heating was playing up, yet again.

Big Ed looked at his father who was now in hysterics. They were in Marion's bedroom and Harry was showing his son how to put the loose coat hangers into a tangle. Big Ed was tired from his efforts but determined to get through these menial tasks and become stronger. He was eager to cause Marion some real harm and teach her a lesson for the way she'd treated him when he was alive. His priority was Val and he wanted to start visiting her to tell her his plan.

'I need to get stronger and I need a body.'

'Steady, son,' Harry was nervous of Big Ed but still felt obliged to warn him. 'Only the very senior demons can possess the living, and even they have to get permission from our master.'

Big Ed laughed. 'I have no master. Nobody tells me what to do and you've seen how they already fear me.'

The torture he'd experienced from Satan's servants had been unbearable and Harry had no desire to incur the wrath of their master. 'Don't do it, Ed.'

He received a punch in response and wondered not for the first time, what sort of monster he'd created.

Chapter 7

Arriving at the military training area in Sennybridge the twins were told they were to undergo a map and compass test to assess their level of knowledge. A run in the hills, some press-ups and sit-ups, to assess their fitness levels, then a first-aid test to ascertain their basic knowledge would follow. The results would determine who would accompany them on their *little outing* as Ryan had called it.

The little jog started pleasantly enough and Ryan bantered and chatted amiably with the twins. As soon as he saw they were in their comfort zone he would stretch them a little further by finding an even steeper incline or upping the pace. Jim and Tony soon stopped answering his questions as they concentrated all their efforts on breathing. They were amazed to see that no matter how many hills they ran up or increases in speed they endured, Ryan was still able to chat as if they were relaxing in the pub. Both knackered and ready to give up, they spurred each other on by look and thought, and the fact that neither wanted to be the first to quit. At the end of the eight miler Ryan was impressed but didn't let on. On physical prowess they'd pass with flying colours, likewise with intelligence so he'd been told. He also knew they were determined. Whether they had the required psychological temperament and common sense he would discover within the next few days. As far as their *special abilities* were concerned, he'd leave that up to the Director and professor at the SAP to determine. Ryan wanted nothing to do with the weirdos who talked about telepathy and visits from dead people. From the little he knew about the twins, he was surprised they had anything to do with that.

Jim and Tony were allowed to relax for the rest of the day and told to have an early night. Both men were clever and were expecting the unexpected so they weren't surprised when they were awoken in the early hours and told to get ready to get close to nature.

'What's the...'

'Three o'clock,' said Tony, anticipating his brother's question.

Fifteen minutes later they were at the meeting point fully ready with head torches switched on. Ryan was impressed. For civvies who had never served, these guys were switched on cookies. The group of six set off shortly after. The three other men were dressed in combats, carrying heavy rucksacks on their backs. As the group got into their stride, the men would banter and make small talk, but clammed up if any questions were asked about their personal life. Although tired the twins were enjoying the experience. Not knowing what was ahead was exciting and for the first time in ages, both felt invigorated and raring to go.

They returned from their *little outing* absolutely exhausted in the early hours three days later, and with renewed respect for the people who served their country. They'd worked really hard and had been tested to their physical limits but from the stories told by the soldiers, knew what they'd been through was a doddle compared to real military training. Told to get their heads down, they were woken at seven am, had breakfast and were packed ready to leave by eight. Ryan accompanied them back to Aldershot where they were to undergo mental agility tests and a swimming test. They would then attend a meeting with Violet Hennessey. The day flew by. Looking shell-shocked they entered a conference room with a long table, at the head of which sat Violet Hennessey. She was studying the contents of two folders and, without looking up, told them to help themselves to coffee then sit down.

'Impressive,' she said when they were settled and she closed the folders one after the other. 'You've passed all the preliminary tests. Now,' Violet folded her arms on the table then leaned forward, toward the twins. 'We have a number of people with your potential but the fact that you are identical twins and have some under-developed talents is what interests me. That, and your relationship with your dead sister of course.'

Shocked that Violet knew, or said she knew something about Claire, stunned them into silence. Observing, Violet wondered if they were thinking the same, and sure enough a surreptitious look passed between them.

They both knew Violet well enough by now to know they couldn't bullshit her. Still, Tony decided to have a go.

'We don't have a relationship with...'

'What makes you think that?' Jim interrupted.'

'Women talk.' She explained that it was easy to pick up conversations between Fiona, Libby and their close friends.

'So you've been following our wives?' said Tony. He knew his brother was as surprised as he was, but would also be aware that the organisation were keen to have them if they were willing to put so much effort into obtaining their personal information.

Violet had no intention of providing further information so ignored the question. 'You already know that if you decide to join us, you can't discuss your employment with anyone. We'll give you cover stories to tell your family and close friends to make your lives easier.'

Jim chuckled and Violet raised her eyebrows and inclined her head. 'Our father already thinks we're spies because of what happened in Algiers.'

'Your involvement in apprehending Ed Walton was what brought you to our attention in the first place.

39

Thankfully, most people know parents exaggerate the abilities of their children. Do you think people will believe your father if he tells them you work for the government as special agents? Really?'

It was a fair point and they chuckled.

'As I was saying, you will need to undergo a programme of testing and extensive training which we estimate will take approximately three months. You may leave the programme any time during that period.'

'And then?' Jim asked the question this time.

'We'll cross that bridge if and when we come to it. Any questions?'

'Is there any point asking for specifics about what will happen after the training?' asked Tony.

'I can't answer that until we discover your true talents, except to say you may be put in some dangerous or at the very least, awkward situations. This will only happen if you have both the skill and desire to do this type of work. If you don't we can employ you in a safer, more academic capacity.'

Neither wanted a boring office job, which Violet already knew.

'Define dangerous,'

'Potentially life threatening,' said Violet.

'And awkward?' asked Jim. Violet ignored the question, sensing the twins were trying to play her.

'Look, this isn't James Bond stuff. A lot of what we do is totally boring but necessary. You may well spend hours watching someone then,' she snapped her fingers. 'Kapow!' It will all kick off and you'll have to act, sometimes purely on instinct. We'll help you to hone those instincts so they become second nature.'

Jim tried to get the Batman image out of his head and to pay attention to what Violet was saying.

'I'll give you a few days to decide whether you wish to continue.' They all knew the twins would carry on with the programme, but Violet had to follow the

40

process in accordance with the organisation's operating procedures. 'In the meantime tell whoever you need to that you took a call from this Head Hunting firm while you were away,' she handed them both two sheets of paper. 'And you're contemplating the job offer. That's all for now,' she stood and shook hands with them. 'Ryan will come and give you some tips shortly. Then he'll leave you for an hour to familiarise yourselves with the information on the paper. He'll ask the questions we anticipate your family and friends will ask to ensure your answers are believable. I'll be in touch.'

'Libby's preoccupied with all that's going on,' said Jim. 'But Fiona's like a terrier. If she thinks something's amiss she'll keep digging until she gets to the bottom of it. What if she phones the company?'

Holding open the door, Violet turned to face them. 'She will be told by a pompous staff member that they are hoping to employ you but any potential contract would be between you and them. If she persists it will be suggested to her that perhaps she should learn to trust her husband.'

'That's a little harsh,' said Jim and Violet replied that an initial harsh response inevitably stopped future interference.

She obviously doesn't know Fiona thought Jim as they said their final farewells. As Violet left, Ryan arrived to discuss the contents of their cover story.

*****

Melanie felt a lot better on the second day and was waiting for Mr Stevens to visit her on his rounds. They'd told her mother she'd been kept in for two days because serious spider bites were extremely rare in their country and they hadn't been able to identify the type of spider. Thankfully, the antivenin had worked but it was a generic one and could have been hit and miss. Mr Stevens hadn't wanted to worry Carol. It had worked, so he saw no reason to cause her further concern. The incident had, however, been recorded with the centre for reptiles and arachnids so they would keep a record of any further incidents of this nature.

The Gazette had contacted Carol and Melanie agreed to an interview as soon as she was better. Unusual for a girl, she hadn't been afraid of spiders before the incident but had now developed a healthy respect for, and fear of them. Mel was already close to Marion and felt an affinity for her that she couldn't put into words. After being told how Marion had probably saved her life, she felt even closer to her. Carol's attitude to Marion had changed significantly. She now agreed her daughter was allowed to spend time with her newly adopted Auntie. The twins and Melanie's father, Graham, acknowledged again that he would never understand the female of the species. Disliking confrontation, and not one to rock the boat, he went along with most of Carol's ideas and was happy for Melanie to spend time with his ex-wife. Graham was a champion weightlifter and had a number of upcoming competitions. Melanie's attack had spooked Carol so if the company and friendship of Marion made her feel better while he was away, he was all for it.

*****

The drive to the hospital had been horrendous; while they were being overtaken an angry driver had opened his window then hurled abuse at them for going too slow. He'd stayed alongside for too long and had a near miss with an oncoming vehicle. Libby knew she and Marion could easily have been collateral damage, and they were still shaken on arrival.

'Everybody seems so angry just lately.'

'I know,' said Marion. 'A woman threatened me yesterday after accusing me of jumping the queue at the auto bank,' she shook her head. 'I let her go in front of me but it was like some sort of invisible tension in the air that people were picking up on.' When Libby shivered Marion put an arm around her shoulder. 'Shall we go for a cuppa? We're early and I'd hate your Mum to pick up on any bad vibes before we even get her home.'

They visited the hospital cafe and felt much better when they went to collect Val twenty minutes later. A man was talking to her. When he turned to smile at Marion and Libby, Marion felt a long-forgotten feeling in the pit of her stomach.

'Hi, I'm Doctor Walters,' he held out his hand for Marion to shake. Libby was too busy fussing over her mother to notice the change in her mother-in-law.

'You must be Marion. Val's told me all about you.'

Marion's mouth was dry. She wanted to speak, but was tongue-tied. She told herself to get a grip and regained her outward composure, though her insides were spinning like a whirlpool.

'And I'm Libby, Val's daughter,' said Libby.

'Err. Yes of course you are,' said the doctor and Marion was pleased to see he seemed as distracted by their meeting as she was.

'I'm very pleased to meet you, Libby,' they shook hands. 'I've given your mother the all clear to go home and the nurse will be along with her prescription shortly. She's probably delayed because we've had an emergency this morning. I'll see if I can find her. Marion?' he inclined his head for her to follow and they entered his office which was just along the corridor.

'I should have said that I'm Val's psychiatrist. Whilst we've managed to stabilise her condition you should be aware that patients can suffer from depression throughout their lives. Whether Val's condition will improve further I can't say. I want you to know this because I'm told she's coming to live with you for a while?'

'That's right, Dr Walters.'

43

'Please, call me Basil.'

Basil, his name was Basil. He didn't look like a Basil. It didn't suit him. She'd think about what name would suit him later.

'But surely she'll get better, Basil?' Marion had a *pull yourself out of it* mentality towards depression so found it hard to believe Val wouldn't improve with time. Although Val had had an awful experience with the evil Gary and her husband's death had been devastating, it had not been as bad as losing a daughter and discovering that your marriage was a sham. Marion had managed to turn her own life around; the Val she knew and loved should be able to do the same, in her opinion,

'It's not as simple as that, Marion. Here's my card. I want you to call me any time, day or night, if you need help or advice. Do you understand?'

She nodded, wondering if she had bitten off more than she could chew.

'Perhaps you should give me your number so that I can check-up on Val occasionally?' He knew this was unethical but hadn't felt so attracted toward anyone since his divorce eight years earlier. He'd had his fair share of girlfriends since, but none that gave him *that feeling* so he wanted to get to know Marion.

She gave him her mobile number then they made their way back to the ward. Walking behind Basil, Marion tried to keep her eyes off his sleek back and sexy butt and concentrated on trying to think about Val, to rid herself of the lustful images that her brain was currently processing. Val was sitting on the bed listening to the nurse who was doling out her prescription. A guilty look passed between Marion and Basil as they both remembered they were supposed to have been looking for the nurse.

Val was eventually discharged with express instructions to both of them that she should have plenty of rest and relaxation, and be kept away from stressful situations wherever possible.

On the journey home she insisted she was well and didn't want any special treatment. 'I've told Carl not to make a fuss so he's not going to make a special journey today, but is coming to see me at the weekend.' Libby had already spoken to her brother and they agreed Val should settle into Marion's for a few days, so there was no need for him to take time off his new job to visit during the week.

'How's Tony? I'm looking forward to seeing him.'

Libby turned to look at her mother in the back of the car. 'He's fine, Mum. But you won't see him for a while.'

She could see the disappointment on her mother's face so hurried on. 'I told you he was bored in his job,' Marion tutted and Libby ignored her. 'And you know that Jim was made redundant...'

'They've gone off to do some training for a new company,' Marion interrupted. 'It's expected to take about three months apparently.'

'They were headhunted by a company called Arbuthnot and Lee who want them to work together as a team. They came to the company's attention through a friend of a friend and Tony and Jim are exactly the sort of people they're looking for.'

'Sounds a bit strange,' said Val and Marion explained that Fiona had thought the same.

'Silly girl called the company and if it hadn't been for Jim doing a bit of grovelling, the boys would have lost this fantastic opportunity.' Marion frowned and Libby skirted the issue remembering how annoyed she had been when Fiona told her. At least Fiona had admitted she'd made a mistake.

Between them Marion and Libby outlined what the twins had told them about the training and their new jobs. They were enthusiastic but Val didn't share their enthusiasm. Their voices faded into the background as she looked out of the window. She was so tired and wanted to get settled into Marion's apartment. She was letting her have the big double bedroom on the second floor. It was bright and airy and bigger than the two bedrooms on the first. She hoped she'd be able to relax there and wondered what her long-term future held. The psychiatrist had told her to take one day at a time and not to think about jobs or relationships until she felt a lot stronger.

Libby could see her mother had switched off and didn't like her expression. She locked eyes with Marion for a second and Marion had a quick look at her friend in the rear-view mirror.

'What is it, Val?'

No response.

'Val?' said Marion, louder this time, but not loud enough to alarm her.

Val brought herself back to the present and gave a weak smile. 'Sorry I was miles away. It's the tablets I think,' she yawned. 'How much longer?'

Marion told her they'd be home soon but Val had already nodded off so they spent the remainder of the uneventful journey in silence.

*****

Claire awoke of her own accord initially feeling rested and refreshed. She touched the area next to her hoping with all her being that Raphael would be there, but she was alone. In that moment the feelings she woke with left her and Claire felt lonely and totally bereft. The longing for her beautiful angel was almost a physical pain and she knew her soul would be an empty shell without him. The bed she lay in was still the most comfortable she'd ever known, but unlike before, she didn't feel as if she were being caressed without actually being touched. Looking around, the room was still a brilliant white but without sparkle and it now felt harsh and clinical. Touching the soft white feathers that made up the wall gave Claire little comfort; it was as if the whole room shared her sense of loss.

She knew she had to concentrate on other matters until he returned. She had to believe with all her being that he would come back to her; the thought he might not was too hard to bear. Claire did her best to dispel her melancholy and considered it strange that nobody had woken her earlier to give her new orders or instructions. Recalling how the enemy's power had diminished prior to her return, she knew something out of the ordinary was going on and she was determined to find out what. Her experience had knocked her confidence and although not senior enough to approach the Committee, the former Claire would have done so. Now she was wary and wasn't brave enough to request an audience, so decided to find Ron and Sandy hoping to discover what had happened whilst she'd been resting – Claire had no idea how long she'd been out of it and was desperate for any news about Raphael. She was also concerned for Gabriella and Amanda, but less so. After looking around for a while she came to the conclusion that Cherussola was devoid of spirits. Her sense of unease grew so she decided to widen her search area and also to catch up with her family whom she hadn't seen for what seemed like ages.

It didn't take long to figure out all wasn't well on Earth. There were many more evil spirits than there had been in the months following her death. In fact, she thought to herself, the only time she'd seen this many evils was when she'd been near Hell and fighting them with Raphael and his mother. Claire observed arguments, fights and people generally being nastier to and less tolerant of others than on her previous visits. She averted a car crash, a pub fight and stopped a

47

burglary, but it hadn't been easy. In each case she was outnumbered by the harbingers of darkness. Even the less powerful evil souls were willing to have a go using the premise that their sheer number would overcome. Claire fought off a number of evils and she was even more surprised than they to have won the battles. Her strength seemed to have doubled along with her skills. While she was safe for the moment she allowed herself a little time to reflect on the situation. She was alarmed that a number of skirmishes had taken place in former peaceful countries and worried about the stability on Earth. Nobody had told her about the infringement at the cave. Trying to figure out the big picture she suspected this had happened but needed to see for herself and quickly made her way there. Sensing the presence of so many evils all about her, she only stayed for long enough to confirm her suspicions. Moving away quickly she wondered what to do next. Her first thought was that there was no point in returning to Cherussola, as there was nobody about to give her instructions and help with the plan she was forming. Then she remembered the unknown angel who had been rescued at the same time. Her second thought was that she needed assistance to fight the many demons. The memories of the battles at the gates of Hell were still fresh in Claire's mind. She knew that although Ron and Sandy didn't have her talents they would probably be able to provide some assistance should she find herself in any sticky situations on Earth. But would they be able to help put her plan into action? She also knew that if the unknown angel was awake, he might be able to assist. Thinking about it he had been in Hell for so long, and had endured such prolonged suffering, that he should be out of it for a long time yet. Even if he wasn't, Claire was curious about him so decided to pay a visit. Her mind made up, she determined the best course of action was to return to Cherussola to find whoever she could to help her.

Chapter 8

Ryan met Jim and Tony outside the restaurant this time. The twins had a better idea of what to expect, but only an inkling. They'd been informed they were going to the SAP School in Scotland. Despite Tony's wizardry on the Internet, his searches had come up with absolutely nothing and his account had also been hacked. Ryan told him later that cyberspace was monitored and any searches relating to special facilities in Scotland, or for SSAP or SAP were brought to the organisation's attention, and the movements of the individuals carrying out the search discreetly monitored. The twins wondered what they were letting themselves in for. The mystery added to the air of excitement and they were intrigued.

After the usual discussions about football and the weather, the men settled into companionable silence in the car and the miles flew by. They had a meal break at Scotch Corner and returned to the car just before four o'clock.

'Do you want me to drive for a bit?' Jim hated being a passenger but Ryan passed on the offer.

'Just relax while you have the chance. I'm happy to do all the driving.'

The twins were bored and Tony decided to have a nap but Jim was too fidgety to do the same. Despite trying to read and get some amusement from his iPad, he couldn't settle at anything for longer than a few minutes. It would have driven anyone else nuts but Ryan managed to ignore his fidgeting and Tony was used to his brother so slept without a problem.

The last hour of the journey was spent in complete darkness as there were no lights as they drove along the winding and hilly roads. Jim was unable to orientate himself to the surroundings. He guessed this was part of the plan. They were somewhere deep in the countryside and eventually Ryan drove down a hill and Jim noticed some lights in the distance. He looked at his watch, almost midnight, and nudged Tony. His brother opened his eyes and ran the back of his hand around his mouth, knowing he could be a messy sleeper.

The lights became brighter and they soon saw the formidable looking building as they neared. Spotlights highlighted the barbed wire, which was being patrolled by big guys in black uniforms who thankfully looked as if they were totally in control of the vicious looking German Shepherd dogs barking at the approaching car. Although the outer-perimeter guard spoke to Ryan as if he knew him, Ryan still had to show ID and look directly into an iris recognition machine. They were expected and were told to park up. Ryan chatted to the man who had checked his ID while the twins were directed to follow two other uniformed personnel into a room. They emptied all pockets and their belongings were placed in plastic bags. They walked through a scanner that didn't bleep but were still told to stand spread-eagled. The guards frisked them and when they were satisfied they carried no weapons, cameras or illegal items, they were handed the plastic bags containing their possessions, then told to return to the car. Ryan drove slowly through no-man's land between the outer and inner perimeter then they arrived at a barrier where he stopped the car. A guard wearing the same black uniform as the first lot, and a belt which holstered a pistol, stepped out of the building which was located next to the barrier. He took Ryan's ID and told him politely to wait at the barrier while he made a call. They saw him take a radio from his belt as he re-entered the building. A few minutes later he returned Ryan's ID and the barrier was lifted. Ryan parked in the car park adjacent to the building.

'We're here, guys. Grab your kit and we'll get you sorted.'

51

They followed the dimly lit path to the front of the building and the door opened as they arrived. They walked into a foyer area that looked as if it could have been a large hotel or corporate headquarters. Ryan approached the reception and the woman dressed in civilian clothes lifted her eyes from her computer screen and grinned like she'd just won the lottery.

'We've been expecting you,' she said standing up slowly.

Ryan vaulted over the desk and enveloped the woman in a big hug, spinning her around at the same time. When he put her down their lips locked in a massive kiss.

Tony coughed. 'Remember us?'

Breaking off the kiss Ryan laughed. 'This is Janine, my better half.'

Janine giggled. 'We haven't seen each other for ages, guys,' she held out her hand and adopted a professional demeanour. 'Pleased to meet you, Ryan's told me all about you. Stand in front of the camera in turn please so I can issue your ID and one of the staff will show you to your rooms.'

While they waited a few minutes for the member of staff to arrive and escort them to their rooms, Ryan explained that Janine was one of the school's permanent staff.

'I offered to do this shift so I could welcome him back,' she nodded to Ryan and grinned again.

'What do you do?' asked Tony.

'You'll find out soon enough. Here's Adam.'

The introductions done they waited while Adam had a quick word with Janine, telling her he'd return to finish the shift now that Ryan was back.

'Why can't any of these answer a straight question?' Jim whispered to Tony who could see how tired and irritated his brother was, so resisted the urge to give a smart-arse reply. Adam called for the lift and entered a code when it arrived. He also inserted a key and the lift stopped at the seventh floor. After a short walk along the corridor they were shown to their rooms, which were next to each other. The rooms had an adjoining door and the twins kept this open so they could chat as they unpacked. The rooms were spacious and comfortable, similar to those in decent hotels. There was a plated cold meal in each fridge and also a few beers. After unpacking Tony joined Jim in his room where they ate their meals and contemplated what to expect the following day. Ryan had told them they'd be collected at seven o'clock so they retired shortly after and despite the uncertainty of what lay ahead, both managed to get a good night's sleep.

*****

Claire couldn't find anyone in authority to talk to so made her way to check on the unknown angel. He was still totally out of it as she'd suspected but as she was about to leave a high-pitched voice made her jump. Her hand flew to her mouth in surprise.

'It's Claire isn't it? Is there something I can help you with, young lady?' he opened one eye and looked directly at her before opening the other. His eyes then flickered around his surroundings before coming to rest on her again.

'I'm Zach,' he held out his hand. 'Charmed I'm sure.'

'Umm, sorry I thought you were still resting,' she said, shaking his hand. 'How come you're awake so soon?'

'I've had years of torture, young lady,' Claire had a problem matching his squeaky high-pitched voice with his authoritative manner. He was also frightfully posh and she tried her best not to look surprised.

He picked up on it straight away.

'Those evil scoundrels did this to me.' Zach pointed to his throat and stood up to stretch. Even

53

stooped over he was very tall and broad which made it even harder to match his voice to his persona. 'Amongst other things, which are far too ghastly and shocking for your pretty little ears.' He closed his eyes again needing to compose himself as memories of the atrocities he'd had to endure flooded back. 'I'm damaged and pretty useless at the moment which is why the Committee has ordered rest until I'm well enough to return to duty.'

Claire thought he sounded well despite what he'd said. 'You do know what's going on don't you?' she didn't wait for an answer. 'And surely you must know we all need to…'

'Hmm. One question at a time, young lady. Firstly, I am awake because I have had years of torture and my system has become used to the deprivations put upon it. Secondly, yes, I am fully aware of what is going on. And to pre-empt your third question I am well aware that we all need to fight the fight but I am in no fit state to take on any evils at the moment, never mind the seriously vicious bastards who I would dearly love to destroy, God forgive me.'

'Are you in a fit state to do anything?' On the return journey her plan had been formulating and now she had a clear idea of what she could do to help in the fight against evil. Claire told Zach her ideas.

'Oh goody. I love a gal with gusto.' They agreed he had a part to play even in his fragile condition, and both went in search of Ron and Sandy. They found them shortly after, chatting amicably on the cream sofa, as if everything were at peace in their world.

Dispensing with greetings and introductions Claire jumped straight in. 'I want you to gather new spirits, I have an idea and if it comes off we might just be able to tip the balance in our favour.'

'Hello, Claire,' said Ron. 'I take it you're well rested? We're both fine by the way except for being worried about...'

'Hello, old chap,' said Zach. 'And it's a pleasure to meet you too, Ma'am.' He gave Sandy an exaggerated bow and she giggled like a young girl. Claire raised her eyebrows, eager to cut to the chase.

Ron started to explain he was worried about Val. As Claire listened they turned as they heard a thud behind them. Zach had fallen to the floor and was in a deep sleep. He was obviously still recovering from his ordeal and needed plenty of rest as the Committee had advised. Claire wondered why she'd thought she knew better than the Committee and assumed he was well enough to help. Sighing she realised her plan would have to wait.

'Shall we see how everyone's getting on?' Ron and Sandy agreed and they returned Zach to his quarters before making their way to Earth.

*****

Val had dreamt of Gary and hadn't slept well at all. It had all seemed so real when he told her he loved her and that he was sorry for leaving her. Annoyed, she'd told him he was a bastard and that the only man she'd ever truly loved was her late husband. She'd also told him to leave her alone and he'd growled and said she'd be sorry. Lying in bed fully awake Val felt unsettled as if the dead man's presence was with her and not a dream. She shivered. There was a gentle tap on the door and Libby entered with a tray containing tea, toast, a boiled egg, some fruit and yoghurt.

'Did you sleep well?'

Val smiled at her daughter, not wanting to worry her. 'Fine thanks, sweetheart. Is that for me?'

'Of course, we'll soon have you up and about and back to your old self.'

Val sat up and Libby placed the tray on the bed. She sat down gently next to it so as not to disturb the contents.

'Are you really okay now, Mum?'

Val put a hand on Libby's forearm. 'It was all too much for me, Libby. I'm not completely better, but well on the way.'

Libby looked down and Val lifted her chin gently so their eyes met.

'I'm sorry for the worry I caused you all but trust me, sweetheart, it's over now.'

Val tried very hard to believe her own words as she spoke but knew she wasn't being entirely honest. She'd be fine while she had people around her and while she was on the tablets, but any thought of her long-term future caused panic attacks and she wasn't yet ready to face it alone.

*****

Claire had observed her mother preparing Val's breakfast tray and noticed she was happy, or as happy as she could be while her friend wasn't well. In fact, her mother appeared to have a spring in her step that Claire hadn't seen since she was alive. Her mother was a giver and perhaps it was because she was helping someone again. Claire didn't over think it as, along with Ron and Sandy, she followed Libby up the stairs and they listened to the conversation between mother and daughter.

'She's hiding something,' said Ron. He knew his wife well enough to know she was keeping something from Libby.

'Well there's nobody here but us and the living,' said Claire. 'Perhaps we should come back later and see if anything's changed?'

They all knew how evil Big Ed was and were concerned for Val's safety and sanity should he make an appearance. Knowing Val was safe with Marion and

Libby for the moment, Claire told the others that she wanted to catch up with her brothers.

'I haven't spoken to them for a while, they must be wondering what's happened to me.'

Ron and Sandy weren't confident enough in their own abilities to fight off any skilled demons without the help of Claire. Ron knew his son would visit Val in the near future and he could catch up with him then, so he had nothing better to do than accompany Claire anyway. As usual, Sandy went along with their plans without protest.

*****

It took a while for Claire to find the twins and she'd only managed it through their requests rather than her own efforts. She'd listened to the conversations with their wives and had visited the company where they were supposed to be training. There was no sign of them and she wondered what was going on. They had called for her on a number of occasions in the past to no avail but as Claire was actively seeking them out she was able to pick up on their request for her company.

Her brothers were honest and she knew they were happily married. At the best of times she was intrinsically curious and decided to have a good look around the building before tuning in for a catch up. Registering the isolated location of the facility, the way it was guarded, the CCTVs and the layout of the place, Claire came to the conclusion it was some sort of secret training establishment. There was no way her brothers were undergoing training for some top-notch corporation and she was impatient to discover what they were really up to.

The twins were shown to the mess hall where a number of people were already enjoying their breakfast. Nobody gave them a second glance and they noted that the other diners were a mixed bunch in age and size. If their accents were anything to go by, they were from all

57

over the country. The buffet breakfast consisted of cooked foods, cereals, coffee, tea, various breads and preservatives. They helped themselves and saw Ryan and Janine at one of the tables. He looked up and waved, indicating they should join them and they made their way to his table.

'Sleep well, guys?'

They nodded and made small talk in between eating. Jim stopped eating and looked around. Both Ryan and Janine noticed a look pass between the brothers. From that moment the twins hurried their breakfast and excused themselves, saying they wanted to contact their wives prior to starting whatever it was they were expected to start on their first day. Hurrying back to their rooms, the twins remained silent despite the constant questions coming from their sister.

'Do you think she's with them?' asked Janine. His look told her exactly how he felt. It would take a lot to convince him. Ignoring him she dialled a number and started talking quietly into the phone.

Mr Smart entered the Control Room and told the staff who were monitoring the CCTVs to switch on the units in rooms 715 and 716. The operative named Isobel looked at him wondering yet again how he'd been promoted to Chief. She was better qualified, more experienced and better suited, yet the hierarchy had ignored that. It didn't help that she'd recently made a few mistakes and the idiot told her he'd *been forced* to put her on a formal warning. She carried out his instructions without bothering to hide her feelings and she barely grunted when he asked how she was. Mr Smart gave up and focused his attention on the cameras. As they zoomed in he was amazed that the newbies hadn't realised their every movement could be witnessed. The only privacy they had were in their bathrooms and thoughts. He chuckled to himself, and even their thoughts wouldn't be private for much longer. He stopped chuckling as soon as he realised what was going on, shook his head and looked at his staff in disbelief. His face was a picture - the sort drawn by a five year old - and the look of disbelief was mirrored on the faces of Isobel and her colleague. Mr Smart called the Director who arrived shortly after with Ryan and Janine in tow.

Jim opened his door and gestured for Tony to enter first. He looked up and down the corridor, followed Tony and closed the door. He heard Tony speaking to Claire and was as keen as his brother to know the answers.

'Where've you been? What's going on? Are you all right?' They generally carried out one on one conversations with their sister purely by thought transference. For a three-way discussion it was easier to speak, and they hadn't been in touch with her for so long that their thought transference techniques were rusty.

'So you're going to be some sort of spies? How exciting.'

'Secret agents actually, Claire, and where have you been?'

'I'm here now so never mind that. Nice to see you by the way.'

'Claire!'

She heard the concern in Jim's voice and was touched. Despite being dead for over two years it was obvious her brothers still missed her.

'Let's just say I was in a bit of bother but I'm all right now.' They pushed her for further information but she refused to divulge the full details, having no desire to literally put the fear of Hell into them, and also knowing that her brothers would be frustrated that they were unable to help her.

'What I can say is that there is a major fight going on. I don't want to worry you but it is imperative that we overcome. Don't be provoked by any angry or nasty people you meet. There's a chance that outside forces could be at work and negative responses could fuel an evil of unearthly sources. Somehow you have to convey this message to all the good guys.' Claire forgot how tiring it was to communicate with those still on the living plain. She was out of practise and also realised she still wasn't completely recovered from her experience at the gates of Hell. Her strength was diminishing rapidly.

'Who's fighting, Claire and what unearthly sources? What good guys?' The twins needed to know more to be able to make any sense of her message.

'I've got to go now.'

'When will we hear from you again?' but as he said the words, Jim knew his sister had already disappeared.

Ron and Sandy had remained quiet while Claire talked to her brothers. They could see she was exhausted and was fighting to stay with it. She lost the battle and they held her while they made their way back to Cherussola as quickly as they could.

The twins weren't the only ones trying to make sense of what had just happened. The Director was the first to speak in the CCTV Control Room.

'My office, now,' he nodded to Ryan, Janine and Mr Smart.

'Not a word about this to anyone,' he said, looking directly at the two CCTV operatives. Isobel was furious. Did he think they were bloody stupid or something? She nodded and got up from her chair, pushing it underneath the desk with a force that was unnecessary.

'I need to go somewhere.'

Mr Smart was embarrassed at her rudeness in front of the Director and intended to talk to her as soon as he returned. He held out his hand and Isobel passed him the USB stick containing the recording. She left the office without another word.

Forgetting about the stroppy woman in the Control Room, Janine gave Ryan a smug look as they hurried silently behind the Director along the corridors until they reached his sumptuous office. The walls were of triple thickness and padded on the inside making it impossible for conversations to be overheard. He gestured for them to sit around the conference table. The Director sat at the head and the space directly to his right was left vacant. Janine sat on the next chair to the right with Ryan directly to the left of the Director and Mr Smart next to him. The Director's PA brought refreshments and left the door open. Not a word was uttered until an older man with sparse curly hair and smiling green eyes entered the room.

'Morning, Robert,' said the Director and the professor said hello to everyone and took his seat on the Director's right.

He could almost feel the excitement in the room and smiled at them in turn noting the confused expression on Ryan's face. The Director was the last one he bestowed his smile on before speaking.

'I take it you have news?'

The Director tried to hide his excitement before answering the question, but this was the sort of event they'd been awaiting, for ages.

'Our intelligence and suspicions were correct. As far-fetched as it may seem, the Sylvester twins do communicate with their dead sister!' he banged his hand on the table and smiled widely at the professor before turning to the Security Chief. 'Run it, Smarty.'

The Director pressed a switch and two panels opened exposing a state of the art large screen with a box underneath. Mr Smart placed the USB stick in the side of the box and pressed play on the remote. Within a few seconds they were watching the recording of the twins one-sided conversation.

'All we have here is one side of a conversation. I don't think we should get too excited.' Even as he said it Professor Robert knew they'd hit on something not seen previously at the school. But he wanted to explore all the possibilities before getting caught up in the excitement.

'What if they're psychotic or delusional?'

The Director nodded to Ryan who had been the least likely to believe that anyone could communicate with the dead. What he'd witnessed in the past few minutes had convinced him otherwise and he had to find a logical reason or his lifelong held beliefs would be proven incorrect.

'We've carried out complete background and medical checks. No family history of mental illness or major criminality. Their sister was killed in a car accident together with the taxi driver,' he opened a file. 'It says here that their wives know they communicate with their dead sister. I must admit that up to now I thought all this was bull but I've spent time with these guys and I would say they're straight up.' He paused, lost in his own thoughts for a moment. The Director and everyone else totally trusted Ryan, knowing he was an excellent judge of character.

'Ryan?' said the Director.

'Tony's wife didn't believe him until...' he shook his head. 'I'm struggling with this so I'll just tell you what it says in the notes. Before they were married Libby, Tony's wife, received a message from her dead father. He was the taxi driver who killed the twins' sister!'

They were all quiet for a moment, trying to get their heads around the information. Professor Robert proceeded with caution, even though he knew the evidence on screen had been pretty convincing otherwise Ryan wouldn't have changed his views. The others were looking at it from an emotional point of view. The professor decided he would be the one to remain rational and trust purely in science.

'I repeat. What we have here is one side of a conversation, albeit by twins who we all agree have no history of mental illness or mental health issues. It's hardly conclusive proof that there is life after death,' he said. 'There might well be another explanation.'

'Such as?' the Director leaned forward, folding his arms.

The professor knew he was desperate for it to be true and hoped this wouldn't cloud his judgement.

'Dissociative Personality Disorder. Unlikely but we can hypnotise them and see what happens.' He looked at the others and could see that Mr Smart was confused.

'It used to be called Multiple Personality Disorder, different voices telling patients what to do. Those suffering from the condition usually struggle with the instructions from different personalities and there have been many cases of people trying to use it as a defence for heinous crimes. Difficult to prove one way or another.'

'But you think it unlikely as far as the Sylvesters are concerned?'

'Director, if we are to trust these men and send them out on missions, we have to be one hundred per cent sure that they're of sound body and mind. Remember...'

'Yes I remember,' the Director cut him off as they all recalled the case of the rogue agent who had caused the previous director to be retired early with a much-reduced pension.

'So will the hypnosis prove conclusive?' asked Janine.

'Definitely not,' said the professor. 'But it will give me an insight into their thoughts and feelings. I'll also scan their brains under testing conditions and will then give my considered opinion. I'd like them to get into the school's routine and carry out the normal programme for now. I want them to think what we're doing with them is somehow normal procedure. They'll be more open if they're not under too much stress, and the results will be easier to read.'

'I agree and think we should proceed with care,' said the Director. He placed his elbows on the table and joined his fingers together before strumming them against each other while thinking. 'We have to be absolutely sure they're genuine, but if they are...'

They all knew that if the twins could really communicate with their dead sister and they could secure her help in the fight against evil, the possibilities would be endless.

The meeting concluded and as the others left the office the Director kept Mr Smart back.

'I see that Isobel's attitude hasn't improved.'

'It's really frustrating, Director. She's just not interested in the mentoring sessions you suggested.' The Director wasn't stupid so Mr Smart knew he needn't mention Isobel's personal grudge against him, or the fact she could be a security risk in her current appointment.

'Okay. I'll ask HR to arrange a transfer and she can work in the archives. Hopefully it's just a bad patch...' he suspected it wasn't but her knowledge on up-to-date operations would be restricted in her new position. 'Tell her the plan and, Smarty?'

'Yes, sir.'

'Don't put up with any nonsense.'

Mr Smart nodded and the Director buzzed his PA, indicating it was time for the Security Chief to leave.

*****

Her mother had been home for three days and Libby wasn't happy with her progress. Val confessed to Libby that she'd dreamt about Big Ed, or Gary as her mother called him, every night and the dreams felt so real she'd woken up frightened. She'd asked Libby not to tell Marion and Libby felt uncomfortable with the request. One of the reasons her mother had had a breakdown as far as she could tell, was because she'd refused to talk about her feelings. Taking her lunch up to her room, she decided to have it out with her as gently and cautiously as she could.

'Scrambled eggs, smoked salmon on toast and a nice cup of tea,' she said as she opened the door with her elbow.

Val sat up in bed. 'Thanks, sweetheart. Not working today?'

'I told you, Mum, I've taken this week off. Marion's gone to see Carol and Melanie so I'm on lunch duty.'

'Marion's an angel to be able to speak to that woman, never mind be friends with her.'

'She's moved on, Mum. It's what people do.'

Val looked away. Libby put the tray on the cabinet next to the bed and opened the curtains. It was tipping down still and the grey clouds matched the way she felt when she thought about her mother's situation.

'Why don't you get up, have your lunch then shower? Maybe we can go for a look around the shops later? It'll do you the world of good.' Libby tried feigning an enthusiasm she didn't feel, already aware of her mother's answer.

'I'm not ready for that yet, sweetheart.'

65

'Mum, please, you have to make an effort. I know how difficult it is, but please just try.'

'That's the thing, Libby. You have no idea how difficult it is and the doctor said you're not to push me into doing anything I'm not ready for.'

Libby tried to remain calm as she wondered why her mother considered showering and dressing to be difficult. All thoughts of asking if she could tell Marion about her dreams disappeared from her head. It was no good talking to her while she was in this mood. 'Shall I leave you to eat your lunch and bring you some magazines to read later?'

Val nodded and smiled, knowing she wouldn't bother to read but agreeing because it would make her daughter feel better. At least she was able to eat some of the food, even though she would puke it up later. Thankfully Libby and Marion weren't aware of this.

Chapter 9

Following the visit from Claire, their first morning at the SAP School was spent rushing from one place to the next and by the time they stopped to take stock, they were told lunch was being served. It had been a good distraction for the twins who were too busy to spend time thinking about the conversation with their sister. They dropped their grips in their rooms and made their way to the mess hall. They'd been given a rough timetable which showed they were to participate in physical training at 6.30 am every morning Monday to Friday – the twins enjoyed keeping fit and weren't bothered by the physical part of the programme. They would do their own runs at weekends, even though it wasn't compulsory. Following breakfast each day the remainder of the mornings would be spent in the classroom with such diverse topics as the current political situation to the best way to break into a building and avoid discovery. IT also featured and Tony expected to be excused some of these classes. The art of disguise and blending in, dress, light cover and deep cover infiltration and unarmed combat were also part of the course. Weapon training, field training and various simulations would take place elsewhere when they were further into the programme. Both were very much looking forward to the *boy's toys* part of the course. Part of the programme was allocated to time with Professor Robert but precise details weren't specified. The twins assumed this was when their so-called special abilities would be tested. They were told that language skills might come later but that for now they would be employed within the UK. Ryan appeared at their table during lunch and told them weekends were for catch up or exploring the local area if they performed to a satisfactory standard during the week.

'Remind me why we're doing this?' muttered Tony as they watched Ryan disappear.

'Do you think we should tell him?' The elephant was now out in the open and Tony considered his brother's question.

'We sure as hell need to think about telling someone here, Jim. Otherwise they're going to think that we're weird or something.'

'Or they'll be testing us to see our reaction to Kryptonite.'

Tony didn't laugh and the brothers became serious. They were incredibly worried about what their sister had said and wouldn't figure out what was going on until they next spoke to her.

'Her message was a warning and I think we're going to need help. Perhaps we should ask to speak to Violet?'

'Let's leave it for a few days,' said Jim. 'Claire might give us another message then we can at least give them something worth knowing.'

Neither wanted to pass on the cryptic message and risk sounding like a vague Medium, or worse, someone with mental health issues.

*****

Deep in the dark pits of exhaustion Claire knew something had changed. Try as she might she couldn't open her eyes, but she felt a warmth that had once been familiar and even in her dream-like state she smiled. Everything was going to be well again.

Despite his best efforts Ron had been unable to wake Claire. He kept thinking about Libby and Val's conversation and was very concerned.

'I seem to spend my entire time worrying about Val these days,' he said to the ever patient Sandy. 'I thought she would recover now Big Ed is out of the picture but something's not right.'

'But you know she's safe with Marion and Libby, Ron.' Sandy knew where the conversation was heading and didn't want to go there.

'If we can move about freely, Sandy, imagine what someone with Big Ed's power can do, especially now so many evils have been let loose and so many angels are missing.'

She didn't respond.

'Sandy?'

'I know, Ron. But we're not strong enough.'

'Please, Sandy. I only want to visit to make sure she's okay. We don't have to get into any trouble with anyone. We'll leave straight away if I think we might be in danger,' he gave his most winning smile. 'I promise.'

She didn't want to go and memories of the way Big Ed had killed her came flooding back, followed by the mental and physical torture she'd received during her short time in Hell. Despite all this she'd never been able to say no to Ron and perhaps he was right. A quick visit - nobody would see them - and he'd be able to stop worrying about his wife if he could see she was making a good recovery. Against her better judgement she went along with Ron's wishes and they made their way to Earth and Marion's apartment.

*****

Claire had dreamed that Raphael was back and she was smiling when she opened her eyes. As she stretched she felt the familiar warmth next to her and thought it was unreal, a cruel residual memory of her dream. It took her a nanosecond to realise that he really was there. She ran her hand along his cheek and he turned his head. Claire saw the nasty wound down the other side of his face and gasped. It looked as if one of

69

the evils had clawed him and the wound was still open. As she touched it, it started to bind together, the healing process speeding up like a film on fast forward. She examined the rest of him and he didn't budge. The wounds were worse on his right side and knowing how exhausted she had felt on her return, Claire knew it would be a while before he would wake up, and even longer before he'd return to his normal self. The fact he was safe was enough for now and she hugged herself. She had to do something to occupy her time until he woke and she also wanted to share the good news with someone, but first of all she needed to check whether Gabriella and Amanda were safe. Claire held Raphael for a while, drawing comfort from the warm familiarity of him. Reluctantly she let him go to find out about the others and to give Ron and Sandy the good news.

*****

Marion was visiting with Carol and Melanie. Thankfully Graham was away on one of his weightlifting competitions. He had flown home when he'd heard about Mel's hospitalisation. Once they knew she was safe, they were happy for him to return to the competition. Mel knew he would lose money if he didn't compete and her mother's part-time job didn't generate enough income for the family to live on. She was also very aware of the fact that if he came home now they would be unlikely to have a holiday the following year. They wouldn't be able to afford the new phone they'd promised her either.

Marion was still surprised she could enjoy Carol's company after all that had happened. Everything had changed since Claire had died, especially her own attitude and she was well aware that life was too short to bear grudges. She and Mel had a special bond and although they weren't blood relatives, Marion thought of Mel as an adopted niece. Mel felt the same about Marion and Carol wanted the best for her daughter so they were all happy with the arrangement. Marion knew she wouldn't be friends with Carol if Mel hadn't been in the picture, but this didn't concern her. She no longer had feelings for her ex-husband and Carol was very welcome to him. She'd only had time for a brief chat with Carol earlier and she'd been told that although Mel had made a good physical recovery since being bitten, it had knocked her confidence and a change of scenery would do her good. Mel returned at that moment and a look passed between mother and daughter before Carol nodded to Mel.

'So, is someone going to tell me what's going on?' Marion took a chocolate chip cookie and dipped it in her cup before taking a bite.

'Well, we were wondering...'

'Yes,' Marion stopped chomping on her biscuit. 'Out with it, Melanie.'

'You know it's half term next week. Well Mum's been offered some overtime at work and Dad's away. I was planning on going to Drew's but she's got a boyfriend now,' Mel rolled her eyes. 'So we were wondering if I could come and stay with you?'

'But the twins are away on a course or something and Libby and I are looking after her mother.'

'I know the twins are away, Auntie Marion, it's you I want to spend some time with.'

'Oh, I see.' Marion was surprised and thought for a minute. Mel and Carol misinterpreted her silence.

'I'm sorry, Marion. I just thought...'

'No need to be sorry, Carol. I'd be delighted to have Mel stay with us,' she looked at Mel. 'But you'll probably be bored stiff.'

'No I won't and I can help you as well and get to know Libby better.'

Agreeing the visit could go ahead, they spent the rest of the time making the arrangements for the following week. Marion's apartment was three bedroomed so she would either ask Libby to move in with Val or ask Val to move to the smaller room and Libby and Mel could share. Whatever they all decided it would be fun and Marion left Carol and Mel with a huge grin on her face, thoroughly looking forward to having Mel for company the following week.

*****

Libby thought it best that she moved in with her mother during Mel's visit. Val's condition hadn't improved and she was keen to help her as much as she could. She was surprised when her mother protested and Marion and Libby had to convince her that Mel needed a break as well.

'She's a teenager, Mum and we hardly know each other. It will be much better if I just move in with you,' Libby could see her mother wasn't convinced. 'Come on, Mum we've shared a room before. What's the problem?'

Val caved in and eventually saw sense. Mel was due to arrive in the afternoon and Libby moved her belongings out of the room and made it ready for Mel prior to her arrival. The three ate a Bolognese for dinner and Mel found it strange that Val's meals were being delivered to her room.

'I thought she was on the mend. Has she got a problem with her legs?'

Marion hid her smile. Mel shared the exact same directness of her late half-sister and she had a point. Perhaps they'd mollycoddled Val too much and it was time for the cruel to be kind treatment.

'There's absolutely nothing wrong with my mother's legs, Mel,' said Libby. 'She prefers to eat in her room and she has been rather tired.'

72

'I'm sorry, I didn't mean to be rude. I have a habit of speaking without thinking sometimes and it's just...'

'No need to be sorry,' Libby smiled at the teenager. 'I think you might be right actually and we should ask Mum to eat with us. What do you think, Marion?'

'Sometimes it takes a new pair of eyes to see exactly what's in front of you and I think Mel's absolutely right. Let's try and coax her down tomorrow.'

That decided they settled down in front of the TV to watch a chic flick. Marion was laughing and joking with them both and seemed full of joy to Libby. It was obvious that she was revelling in Mel's company and Libby experienced a pang of envy, wishing she could recapture that level of intimacy with her mother. She was determined to speed up her mother's recovery and vowed to start the following day. Unfortunately others had different plans.

Val was asleep when Libby went up and she managed to keep quiet enough so as not to wake her. She'd had a few glasses of wine and was tired and slept within seconds of her head hitting the pillow. Libby didn't know what time it was when she opened her eyes and wondered what had woken her. There it was again. She pressed the button on her phone, 03.47 and shone the light around the room. Her mother was lying on her side but shaking her head and groaning while she did so. She was obviously distressed and Libby wasn't comfortable knowing she must be having a nightmare. Getting up quickly, she walked to the side of her bed.

'Wake up, Mum,' she said quietly so as not to alarm her.

No response so Libby gently shook her. 'Mum! Wake up.'

Val opened her eyes and Libby shrank back at the fear they held. Val pulled her daughter toward her urgently.

'He was in my dream again tonight. He won't take no for an answer Libby and says we'll be together again, one day.' She swallowed hard. Now fully awake Val realised the fear had made her reveal far too much and seeing the look on Libby's face she regretted telling her.

'You dreamt about that Gary who died in prison, Mum?'

Val nodded as she wiped a tear from her eye.

'Is this what's been worrying you? You're still having these nightmares?'

She nodded again. 'It's so real, Libby. As if he's actually here and it's not just a dream.' Now that the floodgates were open Val found it hard to stop and she told Libby everything.

'As you know, I told him I wasn't interested and didn't want him any more. Then he got angry and now he just comes and terrorizes me. He told me that nobody leaves him, ever and that I'm destined to be with him.' Val was crying again and shaking as she explained.

Libby sat on the bed. 'Mum, he's dead and can't harm you,' she held her mother's hands. 'It's not really him, it's your subconscious mind trying to make sense of everything that's happened. Because it's too much for you to get your head around when you're awake, you dream about him.'

'But…'

'It could also be the drugs, maybe you should ask your doctor for a lower dose.'

'No!'

The strength of her mother's response made Libby sit back. 'It was only a suggestion.'

74

'Sorry, sweetheart, but I'm not ready for that yet,' Val smiled and ran her hand along her daughter's cheek. 'You're so thoughtful, Libby, and I appreciate that. I'm fine now. You go back to sleep and I'll see you in the morning.'

'I don't like to leave you like this.'

'Honestly, Libby, I'm fine. It's not as if you're going anywhere.

'Well, if you're sure.'

Val said she was and Libby crawled back into her own bed and closed her eyes. She was asleep within a minute. Val was envious as she looked at her daughter, too afraid to go back to sleep in case he returned to terrorise her.

She nodded off eventually, her body too tired to stay awake and he was back. Libby heard her mother groan again. She left her own bed and lay down next to Val. She held her mother and made soothing noises telling her everything was going to be okay. Val eventually stopped moaning and fell into a peaceful sleep. Libby slept lightly, subconsciously listening for any noise, like a new mother with her first baby.

Marion opened her eyes and looked around the room. She sensed a presence like she had when Claire had visited a while back, but she knew this definitely wasn't Claire. The hairs on her arms and neck stood on end and a shiver crept up her spine. The curtains swayed and she knew for a fact that something or someone was with her. She tried to remain rational but knew that an evil presence was in her room. She was frightened. Her memory took her back to Zambia and she recalled the looks from Gary – even though they'd since discovered that this name was an alias, Marion would always think of him as Gary. Even then her sixth sense had told her he was a bad one and now, in the darkness of night in her own room, her mind played tricks and she wondered if he was in her house. Marion shook herself and put the light on, knowing the darkness would only cause her mind to wander further. Forcing her logical side to prevail she muttered to herself.

'There's nobody here but you.'

She knew she was now on her own and tried to convince herself it had all been a product of her subconscious over-reacting because she so was worried about Val. She closed her eyes but sleep evaded her for the rest of the night. She was totally unaware of the chaos about to occur in the void between the next worlds.

*****

Ron and Sandy had heard the entire conversation.

'My concerns were justified then,' said Ron looking down at his wife and daughter and speaking more to himself than anyone else. When Sandy didn't respond he looked in her direction. All colour had drained from her face. Ron now sensed the presence and her expression told him he was right. He turned and looked at him.

'Ho, ho, ho. What have we here then?' Big Ed smiled, clapped his hands then rubbed them together, as if looking forward to having some fun.

Ron's first thought was inappropriate. Big Ed was doing a Father Christmas impression. He snorted and Sandy looked at him as if he were mad. Ron's unexpected reaction threw Big Ed off kilter and Ron took advantage, knowing his and Sandy's combined strength was nowhere near enough to fight this evil monster. Sandy was stunned and incapable of moving of her own volition. Ron grabbed her hand and propelled them as quickly as he could through the atmosphere. It wasn't fast enough and Big Ed effortlessly caught up. Every time Ron propelled them in a different direction and he thought they'd escaped, he looked up to find their tormentor in front of them, seemingly enjoying himself like a cat toying with a terrified mouse.

Ron was quickly running out of options. He didn't need to look at Sandy to see she was terrified but still he grabbed her other hand and told her to concentrate.

'The circle of love, Sandy. Whatever happens to us, just think of love and good memories.' He knew she didn't have too many of those but it was the last resort.

'I don't know if I...'

'Do it, Sandy,' he tried to sound calm and in control. 'We can do this.' Squeezing her hands he tried to convey his strength and hope to her. They closed their eyes and all was calm for a second, until Sandy screamed and they were thrust through the ether at a speed Ron had only known when accompanied by angels. He opened his eyes to see Big Ed pummelling Sandy's face and Ron felt a rage that he didn't know he possessed.

*****

The first few hours with Professor Robert passed pleasantly and the twins enjoyed his company. He wasn't what they'd expected and seemed like an ordinary bloke, neither eccentric nor absent-minded, although highly intelligent and, from their discussions, extremely perceptive. They'd chatted and got to know each other and they felt relaxed in his company. The professor explained that he wanted each twin to undergo a brain scan, which was standard procedure in the wing. There would be further tests and examinations but he would give them more information after examining the results of their scans.

'There's nothing to be alarmed about and whilst the tests are invasive to a degree, there will not be any pain or after effects.'

They agreed. From years of knowing each other's thoughts and subtle nuances of body language, each knew the other trusted the professor and without discussing it, the joint decision was made to talk to him about their sister. Even the professor didn't notice the look that said Tony was going to broach the subject.

'Can we talk to you in private and in confidence?' asked Tony.

'You can certainly talk to me,' he scratched his chin. 'But I'm an employee of this school and if I think you may have information that the Director should know, I am legally and duty-bound to tell him.'

'Who's the Director? Is he Violet's boss?'

The professor chuckled at Jim's question. 'Violet does refer to him as her boss, yes and for all intents and purposes he is. But only when she says so.'

'Ah,' now it was the turn of the twins to chuckle.

'So they're married.'

The professor nodded.

They were planning to talk to Violet about their sister and she had already mentioned to them that the school knew something about Claire.

'If we come clean with you, will you do the same with us?' asked Tony.

He laughed. These guys weren't stupid. 'If I say I don't know what you mean, would you believe me?' Their look answered the question. 'We investigated the way Big Ed Walton was captured and his relationship with your mother and mother-in-law. Then we listened to some of the conversations your wives had...'

Violet had already told them this but they were interested in the professor's view.

'Where?' asked Tony.

'I can't tell you,' the professor put up a hand to stop further interruption. 'Not because I don't want to, but because I don't have that information. We work on a *need to know* basis and apparently I don't need to know everything. What I can tell you is that certain conversations between your wives and their friends were monitored. Your father is very proud of you both and it couldn't have been very difficult to obtain information from him,' he was all smiles again. 'Your father thinks you're some sort of special agents already, as you well know. So do you still want to talk to me?'

'Our sister paid us a visit earlier. You probably know that Claire died in a car crash over two years ago?'

'I'm sorry for your loss.'

'We were extremely close and as you can imagine, absolutely gutted.' The twins recalled their pain when they first realised that Claire had passed. 'Even then we knew she'd gone before we were told officially.'

'We didn't think there was anything strange or unusual,' said Jim. 'We always seemed to know when she was in trouble or needed us; it's been like that as long as I can remember.'

'For both of us,' said Tony.

'As well as the grief, we felt guilty we hadn't been able to do anything to save her.' Jim shuddered recalling the early days after Claire's death.

'We went off the rails for a bit, smoking and drinking too much and if Fiona hadn't got a grip of me, I'm not sure I'd be here now.'

'And you, Tony?'

'We're a team whether we like it or not and when Jim started getting better he dragged me along with him. Our father was ill for a while and we had to look after him. You can't spend time wallowing in self-pity if you have to look after others.'

79

'You may be aware of our, err...'

'Let's just call it unusual family circumstances,' said Tony, interrupting his brother.

'Yes, we are,' the professor was trying to hide his surprise at the revelations. He wanted to know everything from their telepathic experiences that started when they were young, to their psychic communications with their dead sister. He'd heard of instances when people knew when someone close to them was going to phone or had a feeling that something was wrong, but never had he heard of such amazing stories and abilities from people who seemed to be of perfectly sound mind.

'Professor?'

'Yes, sorry. You need to know that we heard you both talking to your sister when you were in your room.'

'What the...'

'I'm sorry but I'm coming clean with you as you requested. We have the ability to monitor all out students' activities without them... without you, knowing.'

'I didn't sign up for this.'

'Me neither,' said Tony. 'What the hell is this place?'

'What you must appreciate is that some applicants are charlatans and we have to weed the wheat from the chaff. We invest a lot of effort in our students. The sooner we're able to discover specific talents, the better we're able to decide whether or not to keep them in the programme. Only once that decision is made do we tailor that programme to enhance those individual talents.'

'So, before you invest any real time or effort in us, or tell us any juicy secrets, you have to ensure we're genuine? And part of that is actually spying on us? Is that what you're saying?'

'In a nutshell, Tony. Yes.'

Is there anything else we should know?' asked Jim.

Tony looked at his brother in amazement. 'He's just bloody told you that they can see everything we do and listen to everything we say, what else can there be for Christ's sake?'

'Well,' said the professor thinking in for a penny, in for a pound. 'We were thinking about taking it a step further and hoping to monitor your thoughts too...'

'What the...'

'Gentlemen, please trust me. You could be excellent assets and have exciting and amazing careers. But first we need to know more about you. I'm sorry but it's the way we work.' Seeing they were eager for more information he continued quickly. 'How would you feel about being hypnotized?'

'Is that it?' said Jim with a deep sigh. 'You nearly had us worried there.'

The professor wondered what they thought might happen but didn't push his luck. 'I take it that's a yes then?'

After agreeing to the hypnosis he told them they'd done enough for one day and he looked forward to seeing them in two days time. 'Hopefully the hypnotist will be able to change his schedule. You may actually recognise him.' Neither took the bait and the professor was disappointed they hadn't asked who was to hypnotize them. Apparently the twins could play mind games as well. Touché!

He stopped them as they were about to leave. 'One final thing. I'm going to request that you are no longer monitored.'

'Yeah right,' said Tony.

'If the Director agrees, I'll ask Ryan to show you where the cameras are located in your rooms and how we disable them.'

The twins left the professor curious to know who the hypnotist was, but even more curious to meet the Director and discover more about the man who could wield that sort of power.

Chapter 10

A quick check had confirmed Claire's suspicions that both Gabriella and her mother, Amanda, had returned to Cherussola. As far as she could tell they were, for the most part, physically unharmed but neither stirred when she looked in on them and she assumed they were as exhausted as Raphael.

Ron and Sandy weren't in their usual location. She'd hoped they weren't stupid enough to go to Earth without backup, knowing that they lacked the strength and power to fight most evils. She searched everywhere else until the only options open were Heaven, a new life, or Earth in their current condition. The only one authorised by the Committee to organise the first two was Gabriella, and she was in no fit state to do so. Claire had a sinking feeling and hoped she could reach them before any real harm was done.

Big Ed wasn't the only one surprised at Ron's reaction. Ron had knocked him for six and he'd hesitated, not sure if he was actually strong enough to defeat them both. Being the arrogant soul that he was, Big Ed fought back, telling himself that a weasel like Ron couldn't defeat him. Ron sensed his doubt and decided to take advantage of the chink in his armour. He fought like a lion and the momentum stayed with him. Eventually the penny dropped and Big Ed knew he could be beaten. He cried for help but his loud cries went unnoticed. Sandy knew she shouldn't be enjoying extreme violence but couldn't help smiling when Big Ed was on the receiving end of a good hiding for a change. The fight continued until seemingly appearing from nowhere Claire was in front of Ron. Despite the violence an air of serenity passed over them and Ron's fury left him as quickly as it had surfaced. Claire did not yet have the power to contain evils for eternity so

Big Ed quietly disappeared to lick his wounds. He added the three to the list of individuals he wanted to destroy, together with the humans that were already on there.

'What made you think this was a good idea?' asked Claire. Ron rolled his eyes defiantly, while Sandy looked sheepish.

'I wanted to check on Val and it's worse than we think,' Claire looked confused so he continued. 'That's how we, err, ran into him. He's terrorising Val and she's already fragile...' Sandy put a hand on his arm and gave a supportive smile and Claire could see that Ron was struggling with his emotions.

'I've found out she's ill because she tried to take her own life, Claire. That business after the wedding and the way the man died was too much for her. She says her life hasn't been worth living since I've left. She started cutting herself and Libby and your Mum found her unconscious in her bathroom. If they hadn't, she might well be joining in this conversation.'

Claire wasn't sure whether Val would actually be with them or the other place but decided this wasn't the time to discuss it. She could see they were exhausted and although they'd won the fight, the battle was nowhere near over. If they encountered any other evils they would surely be easily defeated in their current state.

'Has she gone home?'

'No, she's still at your Mum's. You know Libby's there and Melanie's also visiting at the moment.'

Claire allowed herself a moment to think about her mother, glad she had a relationship with her stepsister and knowing that to some degree Mel was a substitute for her.

'Claire?'

'So Val's safe for the time being?'

Ron nodded grudgingly.

'I know you want to protect her, Ron but in your current state you would be more of a hindrance than help. You know what a vengeful bastard Big Ed is?' Ron nodded. 'You'll be on his list now and if you are with Val, you could actually make it easier for him to kill two birds with one stone so to speak.'

Knowing Claire was right didn't make it easier to bear but Ron knew he had to replenish his energy and reluctantly agreed to return to Cherussola to do so.

'What are you going to do?'

'I can't tackle them all alone and can only stop the small stuff. You know, minor fights and skirmishes, burglaries, perhaps even the odd car crash. I've already helped a few people.' Remembering how she met her own death before her time, Claire was glad she'd already avoided the same misery for a few others.

'You think the evils can cause these activities?' asked Sandy.

'Not can, Sandy, are. So many have escaped that the balance has changed. Anything is possible and I've had personal experience of their powers. All it will take is for one of their leaders to organise them properly and chaos will rule.' She looked terrified and Ron thought she was recalling her own experiences at the gates of Hell.

'Claire?'

Shaking herself she continued and he could see the look of determination return to her face. 'We must try to stop that. Hopefully by the time you're rested and I put my plan into action, Amanda, Gabriella and Raphael will be back to their normal selves, and Zach will be able to join us too.'

'Ah,' Ron noticed the sparkle in Claire's eyes when she mentioned her lover's name. 'So they're back. Are they all right?'

'They're exhausted, Ron, like I was when I returned. We won't know if there's any long-term damage until they wake. I'd be too tempted to try and wake Raphael if I was with him so that's another reason I'm here. As well as saving you guys of course.'

Ron resisted the urge to point out they'd managed quite well on their own thank you very much. He was struggling to stay in control with the passing of each second and he also sensed Sandy's exhaustion. They didn't have much longer before they would be out of it and they needed to be in the safety of Cherussola, where they could come to no harm.

'We'll be off then, Claire. Good luck and stay safe.'

She waved them goodbye and being an optimist hoped by the time they awoke, coupled with her own hard work, normal order would be restored.

*****

Claire discovered the evils were becoming better organised. Whilst there wasn't any pattern to the sequence of events, each individual incident she witnessed was run with almost military precision. She observed a clear hierarchy of evils where each had been allocated specific tasks. The lower echelons would start by causing minor disturbances that irritated people, then their more senior leaders would escalate the trouble. Claire stopped a fight breaking out at a fast food outlet. A customer tripped over an object that was surreptitiously put in their way. At the same time a wallet was moved and to the individual who owned the wallet it looked as if the trip was a diversion for the fallen man's accomplice to steal it. An argument ensued but before the first punch was thrown Claire noticed the fallen man's little girl who he'd forgotten about in the heat of the moment whilst defending his honour. Claire gave the child a gentle push toward her father.

'Ow!' shouted the child and the man froze.

'Somebody pushed me, Daddy.'

Seeing and hearing the child calmed both men and although they would never be friends, they realised that fighting was not the answer. The man who had fallen told his daughter and the girl's mother to take a seat and he strutted down the aisle behind them with his head held high. The other man put his wallet into his pocket and left shortly after, determined to keep a better eye on his valuables in the future.

One of the senior evils hissed at Claire and others soon appeared by his side. She disappeared as quickly as she could and very soon she was at another crisis. This time a traffic accident had already happened. Luckily there were only minor injuries and Claire listened to one of the drivers involved tell a policewoman that both sets of traffic lights were on green at the same time, and that had caused the accident. The policewoman took notes and arranged for her colleague to carry out a breathalyser test on the man who gave her the information, and on another woman driver who swore that this was the case. Claire frowned. Changing traffic lights took tremendous ability and this meant the chief evil in situ was likely to be at least as powerful as Claire. If accompanied by others he or she would be able to defeat her, so Claire didn't hang around to find out. She made her way back to Cherussola determined to put her plan in motion as quickly as she could.

*****

Claire assessed the situation as soon as she arrived. Raphael, Gabriella and their mother were still totally out of it with not even a sign they would come round any time soon. She plucked up the courage to seek an audience with the Committee, but was told to go away because they were too busy. When she asked the chamber guardian if he could put her idea to the Committee he gave her a snooty reply, telling her they had more important issues to deal with than a junior spirit's ideas. Claire tried to maintain an air of serenity and floated off to lick her wounds. So there was nothing she could do she pondered, but yet again she knew they had no chance of winning the fight unless they were trained, organised and motivated. Would she get into trouble if she tried? Claire smiled when the truth dawned. If she didn't try they would lose and all end up in torture chambers in Hell. If she tried and failed the result would be the same. But, and it was a big but, if by some chance her attempts led to success who would complain? She made her way to see Zach. He was still asleep but not the deep mysterious world where souls couldn't be reached. It took a while but eventually she roused him. As soon as Zach opened his eyes he was alert.

'Hello, young Claire. What's going on?' his eyes flickered around his quarters before coming to rest on her. 'Just checking, my dear. One can never be too sure.' Zach would never feel completely safe and occasionally had to reassure himself he wasn't still in Hell. His visual check confirmed he was in Cherussola and he relaxed while sensing the impatience of the young spirit.

'How may I help?'

Zach was impressed with Claire. She'd correctly assessed he wasn't yet strong enough to help her fight any evils or to gather new spirits. He didn't know if it was coincidence or a canny sixth sense but she asked him to do the job that best suited his abilities. She waited anxiously for his response knowing it would be almost impossible without him.

'I love a gal with gusto.'

She exhaled and smiled, lightening the mood for a moment. They both knew the enormity of the task ahead. The only way Claire could cope was to break it down into bite size pieces – she tried to think of it as a large bar of chocolate and each individual task was one chunk out of the whole.

They talked details then agreed they would speak to Ron and Sandy before Claire's departure for the first part of the mission.

They were both just coming round when Claire and Zach appeared and Ron said he felt perfectly fine. Sandy was well rested too, so Claire asked if they were ready to help her and the damaged angel to fight the battle against evil.

'I'll do anything I can to help, Claire, as long as it doesn't involve...' she gulped and Claire knew what was coming.

'You'll be perfectly safe, Sandy.' Seeing the look of relief on their faces she felt a little guilty at the white lie and continued. 'I'm going to bring some new spirits here to train and help us fight the fight.'

'But, but...'

'But what, Ron?' she asked, smiling innocently.

'Err, do you actually have the authority to...'

'Authority to do what, Ron?' she shook her head when he attempted to interrupt. 'The Committee are too busy to see me and I can't sit around doing nothing. Our senior angels are still out of it...'

'I do beg your pardon, Claire, but really,' although it was a high-pitched squeak none of them missed the authority in Zach's voice and he continued. 'Although I'm not yet fully fit for active service, I am able to help and am sure the Committee would sanction young Claire's plan if they knew about it. Carry on, Claire.'

'Thank you, Zach. As I was saying, despite searching everywhere else I could think of I couldn't find anyone else in a position of authority, except Zach, who would give me the go ahead. If somebody doesn't act we'll all end up in Hell and...' Claire mentally crossed her fingers. It wouldn't hurt them to think Zach had authorised the operation, especially if it brought them on side.

'I'll do it, whatever it takes.' Having been rescued from Hell, Sandy knew what awaited them if the evils prevailed and had no desire to revisit.

'When do we start?' Common sense triumphed and Ron trusted Claire even though she could be single-minded and stubborn. Sometimes those characteristics also made her a determined individual who would see an idea through from start to finish, despite any obstacles, or in this case, evils, put in her way. In Gabriella's absence he hoped that Zach would be able to rein her in if required.

'I'll bring the new spirits to you around a hundred at a time,' she didn't say how. 'Under Zach's instruction I want you to work out an induction programme,' seeing their confusion she continued. 'Remember how terrified and confused we were Ron, when we first arrived? Well, I want you to make the new spirits feel welcome and comfortable. Try to remember the questions we had and as well as answering them I want you to explain what happens here. Orientate them so they're used to their surroundings and get them ready so that when I return we,' she nodded toward Zach, 'can start training them.'

'Sounds easy enough,' said Ron. 'But what if they ask us questions about the training and other stuff, how do we answer that?'

'Good question, Ron.'

She's gone into Margaret Thatcher mode, he thought as he listened to Claire's instructions.

'After seeing me and Zach carry out the initial training, you and Sandy will be involved in training the next newbies and so on.'

She explained she would also teach them how to gather more good souls from the ether and bring them to Cherussola.

'Zach will head up the operation from this end and will guide and advise you. Eventually I'll need you to select thirty or so of the first one hundred I bring back. Most of the second part of our training will involve circles of love and trying to teach the souls to endure significant pain and torment, without allowing the circle to be broken. They'll need to be mentally and physically strong.'

They were amazed at the plan and Sandy grabbed Claire in a bear hug, which completely threw her off kilter; Sandy wasn't usually tactile.

'I love you and if I'd ever had a daughter I'd want her to be exactly like you, Claire.'

'Err, I love you too, Sandy.' Claire started giggling and Ron and Zach joined them in a group hug while they all giggled together. Claire's strategy might not work but it released the tension and gave them hope, and for that they were grateful.

'This is marvellous, Claire,' Zach broke the hug. 'But I do think you need to jolly on now. None of this can happen unless we have some new souls to work with.'

The talking over and arrangements in place, it was with renewed vigour that Claire made her way to the ether, where the new souls were pulled one way or the other.

The work was exhausting and Claire didn't know how long she'd been at it. By the time she'd gathered her first one hundred new souls and pushed them in the right direction she was ready to return to Cherussola. She was lucky that the majority of evils were too busy causing problems on Earth to worry about what she was up to. The only resistance she'd encountered had been from minor evils or mavericks who'd floated around under their own auspices. They were disorganised and were an irritation rather than a major concern.

'It's him!' said Jim. 'Whatshisname.'

Tony looked at the famous hypnotist as he approached. 'I don't get it. Do they pay him for this like it's a gig or something?'

Jim and the professor rolled their eyes. 'He works for us,' said the professor. 'We recognised his talent early on but never expected his star to rise so high and so quickly. It's come in handy though because so-called celebs often book his services to help with addictions and other bad habits. If we think they're any sort of risk Donny's always willing to go the extra mile to help us, and his clients are none the wiser.'

'That doesn't sound right to me.' Tony frowned and addressed the professor. Before he had a chance to say more Donny Mindmeld was standing next to them. The professor did the introductions and they all shook hands.

'Mindmeld, really?' asked Jim and Donny laughed. 'Trust me, it wasn't my idea, but it's not a name you'll forget in a hurry is it?'

'Fair point,' said Jim and they all chatted amiably for a few minutes. The professor told them there'd been a minor delay and they decided to have some refreshments while they waited.

'Where's the coffee?' asked Tony and he was told they'd run out. He looked sceptical and the professor knew that with the twins being so astute, it would be difficult to pull the wool over their eyes. They didn't want to risk caffeine overdose and he figured they'd managed to work this out themselves.

The delay was due to the Director's late arrival. Violet, Ryan and Janine were on the other side of the two-way glass; they could see the twins, professor and Donny but couldn't be seen. Following the professor's discussion with the twins they wanted to be honest wherever possible. Unfortunately this wasn't one of those occasions. Had the twins known there was an audience it was likely they wouldn't have been able to relax and might not have gone under. There was a chance they wouldn't go under anyway, but everyone concerned wanted to give it the best shot and the professor assured the Director he would talk to the twins at their next session and explain the reasoning to them. Yet again, Jim and Tony were one step ahead.

'Who's watching us?'

'What makes you think that, Jim?'

They didn't hide their frustration this time and sensing the tension Donny thought he should step in.

'Credit them with some intelligence, Roger. They wouldn't be here if you thought they were that stupid.'

He deigned not to respond to Donny but turned directly to Jim. 'Violet's watching with Ryan and Janine. We're waiting for the Director.'

'We need to talk,' said Tony to his brother and they headed towards the door. 'We'll be back shortly.' Tony closed the door behind them and they made their way to their own rooms, certain this was the only place where they couldn't be overheard.

'What do you think?'

Jim sighed. 'Remember the professor told us they work on a need to know basis?' his brother nodded. 'Well I think they'll drip-feed us information if we ask for it, otherwise they'll keep us in ignorance and use *national security* as the reason for doing so. That and the fact that they've had fakes here before.'

Instead of looking annoyed or concerned, Jim smiled as he finished talking. Tony initially wondered why, until it clicked.

'So we play the game and do the same to them? This could be fun.' They high-fived and returned to the room telling Professor Roger and Donny to go ahead when the Director arrived.

'Let's take a break.' It was a while later and the professor inclined his head indicating that Donny should follow him out of the room. The twins ambled over to the refreshment area and Tony remembered there wasn't any coffee.

'Any chance of some coffee?' he called looking directly at the glass wall area and shaking the empty coffee container.

'Damn,' said the Director and Violet laughed.

'I'll get it.' said Janine and she'd left the room before the Director nodded.

The twins thanked her for bringing the coffee. 'Just in case they're not listening, you best tell them we're not relaxed enough to be hypnotized today, Janine. We gave it our best shot, but...' Jim shrugged.

'We were going to tell you but thought having an audience would make it harder for you...'

'Guess that backfired then,' said Tony as he turned towards the door. The Director, Violet and Ryan walked in followed by the professor and Donny.

'Sorry to have wasted your time,' the Director said to Donny. The hypnotist assured them all it wasn't a problem. He shook hands with the twins and wished them good luck before saying goodbye to everyone.

'If we're going to work together I guess you're just going to have to trust that we're telling the truth,' Tony looked at his brother.

'Saying that, it will be a stretch because even we find it hard to believe at times. Right, what's next?' They were enjoying themselves and keen to get on.

The Director nodded toward Violet, grateful that Jim had given them an opening.

'You said yourself, Jim, that you still find it hard to believe. Well put yourselves in our position,' she didn't wait for a response. 'Before we get into the nitty gritty, would you be prepared to undergo a lie detector test? For scientific purposes and so we can move forward trusting each other as Tony mentioned?'

For reasons unclear to Violet the twins found this funny. 'Yeah, sure. Why not?' said Jim. 'But at some stage you're going to have to take a leap of faith and believe what you previously thought was unbelievable.'

Fascinating and likeable subjects thought Professor Roger as he watched the tag-team conversation and looked forward to doing more work with them.

Chapter 11

Isobel had been called to her boss's office. She knew she'd taken her eye off the ball recently and assumed Smarty wanted to extend her warning. She'd find it hard to take another telling off from him but she'd have to try and keep her mouth shut, knowing it was almost time for her annual appraisal. Isobel didn't expect a very good report but needed to prove herself and stop getting warnings if she wanted to move out of the monitor room and not work anti-social hours any longer.

Taking a breath she knocked on the door.

'Come in.'

She entered his office, trying to hide the look of disdain she was sure must be on her face.

'Ah, Isobel, take a seat,' he indicated to one of the comfy chairs and not one around the table. 'Can I get you a coffee?'

She shook her head. She'd expected an interview without coffee, something wasn't right here.

'Ermm, right then,' he sounded nervous even to himself and cleared his throat before continuing. 'Okay, Isobel. I've called you here today to chat about your performance. How do you think you are doing?'

Isobel admitted her mistakes and added that she didn't enjoy working shifts.

'Firstly, Isobel due to those mistakes I have no choice but to extend your warning.'

She was up to speed with the school's regulations so couldn't argue that point.

'With regard to working shifts, that's not going to be an issue any longer,' he gave a sympathetic smile and she knew it wasn't good news.

'The Director's decided to move you to archives where you'll work days. There'll be on the job retraining of course but this will give you a level of stability that you don't have at the moment.'

Isobel was stunned.

'Do I have a choice?'

'Not if you want to continue working here, and of course we'll review the situation in six months.'

Even though she wouldn't have to work shifts and ask her mother to look after the kids and she wouldn't be tired all the time, the archivist job was the most tedious and boring in the organisation. It was also the kiss of death for her career - there were no high flyers in the archives department. The choice he'd given her was take it or leave it, no choice really and Isobel kept a tight hold on the fury that was growing within her.

Smarty passed her the details and droned on about the arrangements. He also gave her information should she decide to leave the organisation – this wasn't an option as she needed the money. She zoned out, listening to the voices in her head telling her she was too good for this move. She had a burning desire to make them pay for treating her this way after five years of hard work and loyal service.

'So, Isobel?'

She came back to the present.

'Take some time to think about it and let me know your decision by the end of the week.'

'I don't need time. I'll move to archives.'

She said nothing further as she got up and left the office.

Mr Smart closed the door and leaned against it. That had gone better than expected. Relieved, he returned to his desk and carried on working at his computer.

Toward the end of her final shift of the week, before a four-day break, Isobel left work and travelled to London. She'd arranged for her mother to have the kids for a few days and knew she would have to be careful if she didn't want to get caught. At Edinburgh Waverley she did her best to ensure she wasn't being followed. Hurrying into a cubicle in the ladies she adorned a long dark wig and changed from her short skirt, woollen tights and long boots into comfortable jeans and jumper, with a different jacket to complete the look. She left the ladies looking like a completely different person to the one who had entered.

On arrival in London Isobel checked into a cheap hotel under a false name and enjoyed a tasty meal in the restaurant, and a quiet night in watching television. She'd done her homework before travelling and after breakfast the following morning made her way to a bank of payphones around the corner from the hotel. She phoned the newspaper and was initially told the journalist she wanted to speak to was unavailable. Isobel told the operator she would go to a rival paper with her story and tell them that *The Investigator* weren't interested in what she had to say. It did the trick and she gave him just enough information to make him want to meet her. They arranged to do so in a small coffee shop that was a short ride away on the underground. Isobel wore a different wig this time and sunglasses. This resulted in some strange looks in the coffee shop but the waiter didn't bat an eye – this was London after all and they were used to the unusual.

The introductions over, Isobel cut to the chase and explained the reason for her call. Grant Chatham listened intently, trying to work out whether the woman was genuine or a run of the mill nutter. Something told him the former.

'So, you're telling me that somewhere in this country there's a facility being used for something other than the purpose the government are telling the public?'

'Correct.'

'And the purpose of the facility?'

'It's going to cost you?'

Grant took a sip of his Latte and studied the woman in front of him as much as he could. The glasses hid her eyes and the collar of her coat was folded up around her neck and the bottom part of her face. She obviously didn't want to be seen or recognised. He'd had his suspicions about various locations for a number of years and thought it worth a punt.

'It's the one in Northern Scotland isn't it?'

Thankfully Isobel's eyes hid her surprise and she forced herself not to react.

'Do you think?' she laughed. 'Nice try, but like I said it's going to cost you.'

She wanted a quarter of a million pounds, some up front and the rest when the story went public. In addition she wanted total anonymity and further compensation if her identity was ever leaked. Grant laughed. 'There's no way my editor will agree to that.' Not strictly true but it was a game and this was just the start.

'You have to understand, Mr Chatham. I'm risking my livelihood and reputation by giving you the information, not to mention my freedom. You have to make it worth my while.'

So she worked for the government and was a credible source. Grant now thought there might be mileage in the story and told her he'd speak to his editor and get back to her that afternoon. Isobel insisted he leave first and she left the coffee shop ten minutes later.

*****

Val hadn't had nightmares for a week. She was totally dream-free and appeared to be on the mend, well physically at least thought Libby. Her mother had turned into someone she didn't know and Libby was doing her best to adapt to this new woman. The mother she knew had put two fingers up to adversity and got on with her life, even helping others with her volunteer work.

It was Mel's last day with them and Libby, Marion and Mel were going shopping. They tried to get Val to go with them.

'I don't think I'm up to going out, just yet.'

'But, Mum, the fresh air will do you good and it'll be a giggle. Remember when we used to go shopping together when I was a teenager?'

'Bet that was interesting,' said Marion chuckling as she remembered her shopping outings with a teenage Claire and the outrageous clothes she would try to refuse her daughter. It had always been a battle of wills and Marion got a grip of herself, disguising her emotions with some banter.

'I'll let your mother worry about what you should and shouldn't wear, Melanie.'

'That's fine, Auntie Marion. If she doesn't like something I'll just tell her you said it looked good.'

Mel was a lot like Claire thought Marion as she swiped her hand above the teenager's head.

'Cheeky mare.'

They all laughed until Val announced she felt tired and was going back to bed. Libby's eyes pleaded with her mother-in-law.

'Come for just an hour, Val. I'll come back with you when you've had enough. You know you love shopping.' Go on, you know you want to.' She nudged Val, trying to chivvy up some enthusiasm. Her friend sighed as if she had the weight of the world on her shoulders. 'Maybe another time, Marion. I'll see you all later.' She left the room and trudged up the stairs as if walking through two feet of mud.

'She's not getting better, is she?' Mel was thinking out loud but could see the others thought the same.

'Come on then, let's go shopping.' Marion forced a smile and so did Libby but Mel knew they were really worried about Val. She was looking forward to some retail therapy and hoped they'd still be able to have a laugh. She loved spending time with Auntie Marion and Libby but whenever she tried to speak to Val the woman only said a few words before staring into space. Mel knew that Val had mental health issues so she always made an extra effort, trying to be nice. But Val had made it so obvious that she didn't want her company Mel had eventually given up, feeling uncomfortable when she was alone in Val's company.

*****

Claire wanted to check-in with her brothers. She found them in a controlled scientific laboratory environment with no possibility of sensory leakage. They were separated but in more or less identical rooms. The walls were white and soundproofed and one end of each room was glass partitioned. Behind the partition was a desk containing two computers manned by one of Professor Roger's team. Standing behind the partition in Tony's room was Professor Roger and Janine was behind the partition in the room where Jim was sitting. The twins looked like human guinea pigs, with pads with protruding wires stuck to different parts of their heads. The wires were linked to the computers enabling the professor and his team to read their brainwaves. Professor Roger and Janine were in contact with each other and the aim of the test was to discover if the twins were able to identify objects by thought transference to each other. Tony tried to convey the thought of oranges to his brother by concentrating on the fruit in front of him. He imagined the smell and taste of one with the juice squirting out as he took a bite. When Jim was asked what the object was he gave the same answer as he had for the other two.

'I have no idea.'

Janine conveyed the information to the professor and he shook his head in frustration and disappointment.

'Right, let's take a break.' He twisted his head both right and left making it crick, then stretched and rolled his shoulders. It was going to be a long day. The assistants in both rooms unwired the twins and they all decided to go outside for some fresh air. The assistants brought coffee and biscuits and they watched as the twins communicated. As a look passed between them Tony said, 'me neither.'

'Stop there.' Professor Roger said louder than he intended and everyone looked at him.

'You neither what, Tony?'

'I was just telling Jim that I didn't pick up any of his thoughts, absolutely nothing in fact.'

'But he didn't say anything, so what made you say *me neither*?'

'They're on auto-pilot,' said Janine. 'They've had a lifetime of picking up each other's body language and don't even realise they're doing it.'

'We are here, you know.' Jim laughed. 'But I guess you've got it in one.'

'But if that was the case, couldn't married couples who know each other intimately, other twins and siblings etcetera, all do the same? You have to admit that we haven't witnessed it to this degree in anyone else?' said the professor. Janine nodded thoughtfully.

'The force is strong with them,' said Tony, failing miserably at his Obi Wan impersonation and receiving a tired look from Professor Roger. The conversation continued amongst the professional staff while the twins enjoyed their refreshments. They felt a subtle change in the atmosphere and knew they had company.

'Can you take a stroll so I can talk to you in private?' It was Claire's voice and Tony resisted the urge to look up. Jim tried not to look surprised.

'We're going for a leg stretch,' said Jim.

'Okay,' the professor looked at his watch. 'Be back at half-past please.'

They had fifteen minutes to catch up with Claire. They walked down the path trying not to hurry, then changed their minds when they realised they couldn't be out of sight of the CCTV cameras. Walking up the adjacent path the professor and Janine watched as they entered the building.

'Wonder what they're up to now? he said.

'Don't know,' said Janine. 'But something's going on. Did you see the way they looked at each other before Jim said they're going for a walk?

He hadn't but knew that women were sometimes more intuitive.

'Something fishy is going on and hopefully they'll share it with us.' But even as she said the words, she very much doubted it.

'They filmed our last conversation with you, Claire, but obviously they only have our side of it. We're safe here and they're not listening.'

Claire wasn't sure how she felt about having an audience. 'How can you be certain?'

'Just trust us, nobody's listening. Apparently we're unique in being able to communicate intuitively and that, together with your presence, will make us a formidable team.'

'Once we're trained properly, of course,' added Jim.

Their sister was quiet for once but they could sense she was still with them.

'Are you happy to share everything with them?'

'They haven't shared everything with us, Claire.' Tony explained about the cameras and the hypnosis when their mentors tried to hide the fact that they were being watched. 'They're decent people and we have formed friendships, but we're inclined not to trust them because of the business they're in.'

'Do you really want to be special agents?'

'Yes!' They answered without thinking and for the first time the twins knew they really wanted these careers.

'I'll help when I can but I can't be about all the time.'

Seemed fair enough and they nodded.

'Spill the beans. What do you want me to do now?' Claire knew her brothers well enough to know a request was forthcoming.

'Can you help with the tests today? You might actually have some fun.'

Tony laughed and Jim explained what was required.

Later that day when the tests were completed and they'd agreed to Ryan's suggestion of a steady state run, the professor and Janine were in the Director's office, showing him the final results.

'So you're telling me that before the break Jim guessed nothing, absolute zilch? Then after, his record was one hundred per cent?'

'Correct.'

'Then you swapped it around and Tony's record was also one hundred per cent?'

'Janine thinks something went on during the break.'

'They did that thing where they look at each other as if communicating silently, then decided to have a leg stretch. They changed their minds after a minute

104

or so, re-entered the building and went to their rooms in a hurry to do something.'

'Hmmm,' the Director looked out of the window for a moment, thinking. He regretted his decision to stop monitoring the activities in their rooms. But he was a man of his word and he refused to go back on it and risk breaking any trust they had since built up with the twins.

Snapping out of it he returned to the present. 'Would you like to hazard a guess at what happened?'

Janine knew it was far-fetched but on the other hand, they all now believed the twins did somehow communicate with their dead sister.

'Well, I wondered if their sister paid them a visit and told them what to say.'

'So let me get this straight. You think that their dead sister flitted from room to room telling them what objects were on display.'

'Yes,' said Janine in a whisper, now wishing that she'd kept her mouth shut.

'Roger?'

'Well. We know what happened in their room so it's not exactly a massive leap of faith to make this assumption.'

'And what did the twins say?'

'They said that they concentrated and discovered they have got hidden talents. But it wouldn't take a genius to realise they were taking the piss and trying to play us at our own game.'

'Or perhaps there's a reason why they couldn't tell us it was their sister helping,' said Janine preferring to believe the twins were now completely on side. The Director knew she generally saw the best in people but he thought this was unlikely.

'We won't worry too much about it at the moment. Just accept the results and do everything in your power to gain their trust. And by that I mean be honest with them.'

'Complete honesty, sir?' said Janine. Both she and Professor Roger were stunned when the Director nodded his head, giving them authority to divulge top-secret information to the newbies, which was unprecedented in their experience.

'But, John...'

'I know what I'm doing, Roger and if it goes pear-shaped, the buck stops here.'

They left the Director's office with a renewed sense of how important the twins were, and curious as to what missions were in store for them in the not too distant future.

Chapter 12

The drive from London to Northern Scotland seemed never ending to Grant Chatham. They'd discussed whether he should fly and pick up a hire car but had decided against it. If he was caught snooping around and the car damaged it could bring further unwanted attention to the paper. One of the paper's affiliate companies had a vehicle fleet and Grant was given a sturdy four-wheel drive vehicle, capable both on and off road and with good acceleration in case of a hasty retreat. It was fun to drive but the journey had become tedious, until he reached the Highlands that was and the landscape changed completely. It had been ages since he'd been out of the city. Grant kicked back and enjoyed the beautiful scenery, feeling his body relax and the stress leave his system as he did so. With Nickelback blasting out of the speakers and not another car in sight, he felt as if he were on holiday and not an assignment – time to get serious about that later. According to the maps and satnav the nearest village was thirty-seven miles from the facility and the place was tiny without a B&B. Naively Grant had thought he'd be able to stay upstairs in the pub but the so-called pub was a one-roomed affair. When he walked in he could have been in a scene from *An American Werewolf in London*. The four old men looked up at him from their drinks and the old woman behind the old-fashioned bar put down her knitting.

'Yes, son. What can I get you?'

'Half pint of lager?' he asked and the woman laughed.

'We may be a bit small and off the tourist trail, son. But we have a full selection of drinks.'

Grant smiled gratefully and asked the woman for directions to the nearest hotel. His face dropped when she told him it was a twenty-five mile drive to the town and there were a few hotels there and B&Bs.

'They are on the tourist trail though, son, so beds don't come cheap.'

He thanked her and sipping his drink, asked about the secure facility for the criminally insane.

'I'm only sorry that it's not further away. Nobody's escaped but you never know, son. Do you?' she picked up her knitting. 'The less I know about that place and what goes on in there the better.'

He finished his drink and left shortly after. The woman went to the window and watched the car drive away before addressing one of the old men.

'Keep your hands off the stock, Hamish I'll be back in ten minutes.' She took her mobile phone out of her pocket and made her way out the back where there was a better signal.

*****

Claire stayed with the twins on and off until the following week when they were told they were to move to Aldershot for a weapon handling course and some field training. They would then have a break before phase two of their training began back at the school.

Before they left the school they were given a story to tell their wives and Claire was at her mother's house when Libby received the call almost two weeks later.

'Yeah, Tony's coming home.' She ran into the kitchen where Marion was preparing lunch. Her mother-in-law stopped what she was doing and turned to face Libby.

'He'll be home tomorrow and so will Jim.'

'For good? Have they finished?

'No, Marion. They're only home for a week. Can I ask a favour?'

Knowing what was coming Marion pre-empted the request. 'Of course, you must go home but only on

108

the condition that you all come round for dinner one night.'

Libby hugged her mother-in-law but then her smile turned to a frown. 'Do you think Mum will be all right with it?'

'She'll be fine,' said Marion, not believing her own words. Val was so concerned about her own wellbeing these days that she rarely considered the feelings of others. She was becoming so self-obsessed that it annoyed Marion who also felt that she could do with a break from her.

'Actually, Libby, I wondered if you'd mind if I had a little break from your mother when you come back?' She held her breath for a second. She hadn't told anyone about her friendship with Basil and if she could get away for a few days they might be able to get to know one another a bit better.

Libby was taken aback by the request but when she thought about it, figured Marion must need a break as much as she did; more so in fact. Marion was such a good friend to her mother that they often took her for granted. Libby knew she could actually ask Val to leave at any time and that would mean she'd have to look after her mother on her own.

'I want to go away for a few days.' Marion added, hoping her daughter-in-law wouldn't ask too many questions.

'Is there another reunion with your Yorkshire friends?'

So it wouldn't even occur to her that a man might be interested thought Marion sadly. She hid her disappointment.

'Yes, that's right, and I'll need a rest by then having looked after your mother on my own for a week.'

'No problem, Marion. It'll do us all good to have a break.' The charismatic psychiatrist had said to be patient, as it would take a while for her mother to get better. He'd also said they should encourage her to do things for herself and to be up and about. Despite their best efforts her mother had insisted on staying in the house and had more or less stayed in her room. As much as she'd enjoyed Mel's company Libby was grateful she'd left and she no longer had to share a room with her mother. It had felt claustrophobic for the most part.

*****

Dressed like a hiker out for a long walk, Grant parked the car a few miles from the school and walked the rest of the way. He intended to find a tree to hide behind and take a number of photographs using the long-range lens on his state of the art camera. The long, boozy lunches had taken their toll and Grant realised how out of shape he was after only one mile. He was sweating profusely and huffed and puffed up the hills. The second mile should have taken him fifteen to twenty minutes but it was thirty minutes later that he found a spot to take some photos. When he'd finished snapping his first lot he opened his bag and took out his flask. After the coffee was poured he rummaged for his sandwiches and attacked them as if he hadn't eaten for a week, even though he'd had breakfast only a few hours earlier. It was going to be a long day and night and he knew he'd need all his energy.

'Got him,' said one of the guards on duty in the guardhouse. The supervisor took a look through the binoculars and checked the photograph on his desk. He was almost certain it was the same man and he phoned Mr Smart who arrived shortly after. They took a number of photographs of the journalist. Mr Smart leaned back, satisfied with their work.

'What do you want us to do now?'

110

'Monitor his movements and get one of the guards with dogs to frighten him away if he gets too near the perimeter fence. There are plenty of warning signs so a good talking to should do the job. If he doesn't take a hint I'll take it further.'

The Supervisor nodded and Mr Smart left to brief the Director.

Grant returned the camera, flask and sandwich rubbish to his rucksack then put the bag onto his back. He got up and stretched, his joints aching from sitting for a while in the same position. He couldn't get a signal for his phone so instead of discussing the next step with his editor, he decided to take a walk to the perimeter fence and try his luck with one of the guards.

There was no need for an announcement that the journalist was approaching as his movements had been monitored since his earlier arrival. The German Shepherd started barking and the expert dog handler held tightly onto the chain. Approaching the outside fence Grant adopted his best American accent.

'Hi. Boy it's cold up here,' he rubbed his hands together and smiled. 'What is this place?'

'Sir,' the guard raised his voice to be heard over the barking dog. 'This is a high security psychiatric facility for the criminally insane.' The guard pointed to the sign showing that entry was forbidden to non-authorised personnel and that trespassers would be prosecuted.

'How many *patients* do you have in here?'

'Sir, I don't have that information. Should you require further information you may write to the Director in accordance with the Freedom of Information Act.'

'And he'll tell me everything I want to know eh?' Grant laughed. Before the security guard answered the question he started to take his camera out of the rucksack.

The guard pressed a button on his jacket and spoke into his radio.

'For security reasons cameras are not permitted, sir. I must ask you not to take any photographs.'

Grant knew very well that he was pushing his luck, but wanted to see how far they would go. Two other guards appeared within a matter of seconds and his camera and bag were confiscated. Another guard who dragged along a ferocious looking dog soon accompanied them. This one came through the gate and growled at Grant who leaned against the fence. One of the two guards without dogs walked away with Grant's bag and camera and the other stayed with him. He thought it unusual they didn't take him into a room to be searched or even call the police, as had happened when he'd tried to enter another high-security psychiatric facility down south. Maybe the procedures were different in Scotland, but he doubted it. Grant's bag and camera were eventually returned and he was escorted to a vehicle by two guards. Thankfully without the dogs.

'Where are you staying, sir?'

Grant had no intention of telling them and asked to be dropped at the nearest village. They gave him a little warning before letting him out of the car. 'This time, sir, we don't intend to press charges. But should you try and breach any of our security in future...' he smiled and left the rest to Grant's imagination.

'You have a nice day now.'

Grant left the car and waited for it to disappear before going into the pub and speaking to the woman he'd met the previous night.

'Any idea where I can get a taxi around here? I've left my car some miles away?'

'Are you all right, son? What's happened?'

'I thought I could walk further than I can,' he shook his head and did his best to look annoyed. 'I'm obviously not as fit as I thought I was.'

'Come on then, son. I'll give you a lift and you can tell me why you're really here.'

She was very astute and he accepted her kind offer of help but had no intention of telling her anything he didn't have to.

By the time he'd collected his car and returned to the hotel Grant was exhausted. He slept for a few hours then called his editor who told him to return to London the following day. Now that they knew the lay of the land the editor would allow him to pursue the story, but with caution. Grant's radar convinced him the facility wasn't what it purported to be and he planned to carry out as much research as he could before returning for another look. In the meantime his editor had agreed to let him publish a general story about similar facilities throughout the country and to request comment from members of the general public – this was always a good way of getting others to do some work and would save time. They'd paid Isobel a small sum so far but she would need to provide more information, together with concrete evidence, in order to receive any further cash.

Fully rested the next morning and with a hearty Scottish breakfast inside him, Grant started the long return journey to London. His car broke down on the outskirts of Edinburgh so he phoned the office to arrange recovery.

'They're asking what's wrong with it, Mr Chatham?' said the girl on the phone who sounded like she wouldn't know what day it was, never mind anything else.

'I'm not a f...' he took a breath. 'I'm not a mechanic, sweetheart. Just tell them it made a funny noise and started shuddering. I managed to get it to the layby before it packed in completely.' He gave her his phone number and location and made her repeat the number, even though it was probably displayed on her phone in the office. 'Can you ask them to come quickly, it's bloody freezing here!'

After they hung up Grant paced up and down, rubbing and thumping his arms in an attempt to get warm. If he sat in the car he was cold and if he moved around outside he was cold. He felt as if the wind was cutting through his clothes straight to his bones and couldn't have been more relieved when the recovery truck pulled up. It seemed like he'd been waiting ages but it had only been twenty minutes. In the warmth of the recovery vehicle the driver asked him if he would like to stay in a hotel the driver could recommend and wasn't far away. Grant did think about getting the train to London but the mechanic's estimate was that they'd get the car fixed and ready for him by morning. He'd explained the fault but it could have been quantum physics to Grant and he wasn't interested. They'd replace the part and it would be fine for the remainder of the journey.

He arrived and was glad to see the hotel was large and appeared cosmopolitan. He contacted his editor to update him on the day's events. It was later on that evening when Grant had eaten a pleasant dinner and was enjoying an after dinner drink in the bar that he was wowed by the woman who stood next to him. He watched as she ordered a drink.

Chapter 13

Claire returned to Cherussola buoyed up and determined having witnessed the worsening situation on Earth. She found Ron and Sandy and was informed the induction of the newbies had gone well. Some were ready to help gather new souls. Claire accompanied Ron, Sandy and fifteen of the newbies to the gathering and instructed them on how to select and assist the newly dead on the first part of their journey. While Sandy and the newly trained went about their business, Claire wanted to ensure that Ron could fight off the minor evils without her assistance. She was sure he'd be able to handle it after his run-in with Big Ed and she wasn't disappointed. As long as he didn't have to supervise Sandy and the others he could deal with minor incursions. She might have to arrange for someone to assist him if and when the evils became organised in this area. Sandy wasn't an option for this task as she generally froze when confronted by any type of violence. Claire decided she had enough to do for the time being and would worry about other issues only when they arose. Returning to Cherussola with another hundred new and confused souls, she gave them a quick welcome talk and passed the baton to Ron and Sandy.

Leaving them to it Claire went in search of the earlier arrivals. She selected seventy and told them to gather around her and prepare to move. She explained the nature of the mission. Though frightened and nervous, they knew they had no other choice but to try and assist.

The mission was a disaster.

*****

Jim arrived home earlier than expected and surprised Fiona. She heard the car pull up and ran out of the front door, straight into his arms.

He dropped his bag to the ground and the impact of her hug sent them both backwards. 'Whoa!'

'I've missed you so much,' said Fiona as she squeezed her husband tightly. 'Where's the rest of you?'

'You too, Fi, but I need to breathe. And I've been working out so I've lost a bit of weight, that's all.' She gave him a big kiss and let him go so they could go inside. 'I want to know all about your trip, but before that...'

Jim knew that look and couldn't have wished for a better welcome home.

They had a wonderful week and the night before leaving arranged to have dinner with their mother, together with Tony and Libby.

Marion opened the front door and scrutinised her sons. 'Look at the state of you two! Don't your wives feed you?' she said, only half joking.

'I know, Marion,' said Fiona. 'I was as gobsmacked as you when I saw Jim.'

The greetings over Marion loosened her hug on Jim and leaned back, still holding his arms. 'Seriously, son what have they done to you? And you Tony?' she let him go and they followed her into the lounge. 'Come on in and tell your mother all about it.'

They all laughed and the twins shook their heads. Now in their early thirties they wondered if their mother would always treat them like five year olds.

'Mum, we're away from our wives, we've...'

'So you're not eating properly just because you're not home. I thought...'

'Jim didn't mean that, Mum,' Tony interrupted. 'We're away from home and have some spare time in the evenings. As we've already explained to Libby and Fiona we're working out a lot, instead of going down the pub every night and drinking ourselves into oblivion.'

Jim flexed his biceps and Fiona gave one a squeeze and laughed suggestively. 'There are a few bonus side effects too.'

'Eew, too much information, Fiona,' said Marion but she joined in the laughter. It was good to see her boys and she was so lucky to have two lovely daughters-in-law.

'I'm going to pop up and see Mum. How is she?'

The laughter subsided quickly when Marion explained she'd been able to coerce Val to join her downstairs for one meal, but other than that, Val wouldn't leave her room unless it was to use the bathroom, and she point blank refused to leave the house.

'The nightmares have come back, Libby. I'm really worried about her.' Marion wasn't sure whether this was the right time to voice her concerns, but once she'd started she couldn't seem to stop. 'She says it's that awful Gary, Big Ed again, appearing in her dreams,' she whispered as if it were a big secret. 'I don't know what more I can do to help her.' Marion didn't tell them about her own experience when she'd sensed something evil in the apartment. It was too much of a stretch and far too frightening to imagine that both were connected.

The twins were concerned and hoped it was Val's fragile mental state causing her nightmares and nothing more sinister. Fiona noticed the look that passed between them and felt smug. They thought they could get away with so much but she knew they were up to something. She was certain there were no other women involved so it was to do with their new jobs. She knew she couldn't contact the company and hadn't yet decided on the best course of action to catch them out. Maybe she should follow them when they returned and take it from there? Libby's voice broke through Fiona's scheming.

'Maybe I should speak to her psychiatrist?' Libby was at her wits end and didn't know what else to do.

'Err, I've already done that, Libby and he said to make an appointment for Val to see him. When I told her she refused point blank.'

'And I don't suppose they do house calls?'

'Actually no, but...'

Well, well, well, thought Fiona as she noticed Marion's blushes. She now watched and listened avidly.

'Because I was desperate and he was, umm, passing this way anyway, he popped in.' Marion explained Val had talked to him and he'd upped the dosage of her anti-depressants.

'He said they'd take at least two weeks to kick-in.'

Libby made her way up stairs and told Tony she'd give him a shout if her mother was awake and ready to see him. He muttered okay but couldn't help wondering if tough love was needed now. They all seemed to pussyfoot around his mother-in-law and he could see it was taking its toll on Libby. He knew it was selfish but he was glad he was away from it and hoped her new tablets would aid her recovery sooner, rather than later...

Fiona was lost in her own thoughts. She could see she was the only one who'd picked up on Marion's body language when she talked about the psychiatrist. She hid her smile while they were all being serious about Libby's mother. It was awful but worse things had happened to other people. Fiona, with the confidence of a successful and happy woman in her late twenties, didn't understand why Val couldn't shake herself out of it and get on with her life. Looking at Marion whose marriage had been a lie for a number of years and who had lost a beloved daughter, Fiona's heart went out to her. She loved and admired her mother-in-law and if she had a second chance at happiness, hoped that she would grab it with both hands. But a psychiatrist? Now that was a turn up for the books.

'Fiona. Fiona, is there anybody there?'

'Sorry I was miles away.'

Marion asked how she was getting on without Jim and Fiona gave her a run down of her work and social life. The twins went to the kitchen to get a beer while the women were talking.

Claire, Claire. They called for their sister using all their mental strength, hoping she'd visit Val and confirm the source of her dreams. Claire was too busy trying to save both worlds so didn't hear their pleas.

The boys returned to the lounge. It wasn't the first time they'd called for their sister and she hadn't turned up. They knew she was busy so would have to wait until she decided to pay a visit on her own terms. The evening continued pleasantly with the party catching up on events and enjoying each other's company. They avoided further discussion about Val, despite the fact that she'd refused to see her son-in-law and her depression was a major cause of concern.

*****

A fight had broken out between two opposing gangs in the town and when the police intervened, the gangs came together against a common enemy. A riot ensued and the police were trying to stop the looting from a number of shops on the high street. Claire observed that the leader of the evil spirits had done her work and now appeared to be relaxing whilst watching the police struggle to restore order. Every now and then when she thought the police were winning the battle

119

and calming the situation, the leader issued further instructions to her minions. They would cause more disruptions and the gang members, without even knowing evil spirits were manipulating them, would resume their violence. The police had summoned extra personnel but were still struggling. Claire could see they were baffled and judged they would have to back off if the situation escalated. It was time for intervention.

Claire looked at their leader and the female morphed into her human form. She was dressed as a Goth. Chewing gum, she blew a big bubble, burst it, put it back in her mouth and continued chewing. Claire instructed her assistants to form a circle, close their eyes and to concentrate on love and pleasant memories, as they had practised. She kept her own eyes open as they drifted toward the evils. The Goth raised a fist and waved it at Claire. She then unclenched it and looking down beckoned one of her minions with her index finger. The weaker evil looked petrified as he hurried to her side as quickly as he could. The Goth smiled at Claire and using the same finger that had beckoned him, she flicked him. Claire watched in horror as the evil sped toward her circle. Speaking with an authoritative voice but in a calm manner she didn't feel, she told her assistants to double their efforts and, whatever happened, to keep the circle intact.

The impact made the circle shudder but when it broke they followed Claire's instructions and reformed as quickly as they could. She had lost one of her number but Claire was proud of the way the others had reacted and felt confident that if they held their nerve, they could overcome. She was looking forward to dealing personally with the Goth. The second impact didn't break the circle but a few of the good spirits couldn't resist opening their eyes. They panicked when they saw they were outnumbered and all thoughts of love and kindness disappeared. This was the catalyst for disaster and when Claire witnessed a number of her students being disposed of one after another she had to admit defeat.

'To me!' she shouted lifting her arm into the air like a tour guide summoning her day-trippers, and the remainder rushed to her side at warp speed, buoyed on by terror.

She concentrated as hard as she could and launched her group upwards. Eventually they were out of harm's way and arrived in Cherussola shortly after. When Ron counted he discovered that eighteen were missing and this weighed heavily on Claire. Tired from her efforts she knew she had to replenish before deciding what to do next. Claire made a speech mourning the loss of the eighteen but assuring the others they would be found and returned to Cherussola. The newbies were understandably terrified by their ordeal and they clung to Claire's words. Looking at them she knew it would be pointless to take them on any future missions. The damage had been done so she made her way to her quarters, head down and totally demoralised.

Lying next to Raphael she hoped her presence would wake him. He didn't stir and it took Claire's mind off her other problems for a moment. He must have endured so much more than she had to still be dead to the world. She laughed cynically as she thought of her turn of phrase, then cuddled up to Raphael reaching oblivion not long later.

*****

Grant tried not to stare at the woman's long legs. Her skirt was short; this was Scotland for Christ sake, she'd freeze if she was going out in those clothes. She sat down on the bar stool next to his and crossed her legs. Her skirt rode even further up and Grant had a tantalising view of the suspenders at the top of her thigh.

121

'Hello, my face is here,' she laughed as she reached over and lifted his chin with a finger. Grant was mortified.

'I do beg your pardon, how rude of me…'

'Do not worry, it happens all the time.' The barman brought her drink and she took her purse out of her bag to pay.

'Here, let me. It's the least I can do.' He gave the barman a twenty before the woman could protest.

'Thank you.'

He knew she was Eastern European but couldn't precisely identify her accent.

'So what brings you to Scotland?'

Her smile disappeared. 'To finalise divorce proceedings. My husband is Scottish and we are no longer friends. I want to ensure that all my belongings are returned. And you?'

Grant explained he was on business and they chatted amiably over a few more drinks. Her name was Svetlana and she was exquisite. Grant felt an irresistible chemistry between them. As they talked, thoughts of his long-term partner in London faded and he wondered if there was any chance Svetlana would spend the night with him. This had never happened to him before and he was mesmerised. He knew he'd throw caution to the wind just to touch that exquisite body. Nobody would know so what harm could it do?

They finished their drinks and Grant was about to summon the barman to order another round. Svetlana leaned over and put her hand on his. 'I must go, Grant.'

She noted his look of devastation and knew she'd hooked him completely. She'd caught the slimy wriggling little fish and intended to play with him for a while before throwing him back in the water. It had been too easy and she hid her disgust well. It was a job after all and all he'd had to do was to say no. There was still a chance that he might.

'I don't do this sort of thing, Grant, but there is something between us. No?'

He didn't trust himself to speak, so nodded.

'Will you spend the night with me?'

Grant felt like his Fairy Godmother had waved her magic wand and offered no resistance when she gently pulled him off the stool. Holding his hand she led him to the lift. Once inside she kissed him passionately, giving him a taste of what he thought was to come. It was as far as she would go but that wasn't what was going through Grant's mind.

He made it so easy for her. As soon as they entered her room Grant asked to use the bathroom. She prepared the drinks, dropped the drug into his glass and gave it a vigorous stir before he returned.

The following morning Grant woke up with a hangover from hell and a note on the bed. *Thank you, Svetlana x*

He returned to his own room trying to recall what had happened. His car arrived and following a hasty breakfast Grant checked out. An hour into the journey his phone rang and the display showed it was his editor. Grant pulled over. His sixth sense told him that the shit had hit the fan and he wondered what he'd done.

*****

After a brilliant week off with their wives the twins were travelling back to Scotland refreshed and ready for their next challenge. They were travelling to Inverness by train where Ryan would meet them at the station and drive from there. The three o'clock train was scheduled to arrive at Inverness at ten past eleven so they expected to arrive at the school after midnight. Waiting at King's Cross for the signal to board the train, Tony thought he saw a familiar figure as he people-watched the crowds. Remembering his training his glance didn't linger. The woman's red hair was just visible under the folded up collar of her mac and she was wearing large sunglasses. She'd blended back into the crowd and Tony wracked his brains trying to think why she looked familiar. It must have been a movement as there wasn't enough of her face to recognise.

'What's up, bro?'

'Nothing.'

Jim raised his eyebrows.

'Okay. I thought I recognised someone over there,' he pointed but the woman was long gone. 'By the way she moved…' he thought for a moment. 'Actually, Jim, I've got a feeling she was dressed in a disguise.'

'Nobody knows what we do. Why would someone disguise themselves from us?'

'No idea and I could be completely wrong,' he laughed and leaned over to his brother, whispering in his ear. 'All this special agent stuff must be going to my head.' The platform opened and chuckling away, they made their way onto the train.

*****

'Are you fucking stupid! How could you let yourself get into that situation? You're supposed to be a journalist for fuck's sake. We witness people in compromising positions, not the other way around.'

Grant couldn't believe what had happened. He knew that all wasn't well but if it was like the editor said, he'd had it.

'How bad are they?'

'Well put it this way, I now know you have a strawberry shaped birth mark on your arse and that you like threesomes.'

'Threesomes?' oh shit. This was worse than Grant could have imagined. 'Come on, Bill, I've obviously been set-up here. Somebody's just trying to keep us quiet. You must realise that?'

'All I know, Chatham, is that you've put yourself in a compromising position and I have no control over where and when these photographs are going to be published. I can't risk the credibility of our paper and anyway, the owner's received a copy - to say he's bloody furious is an understatement. I'll get your stuff delivered to your house, I don't want you anywhere near these premises again. Do you understand?'

Grant was angry, upset and also incredulous that Bill would sack him when he thought they were friends. Even though it was obvious he'd been had, his boss had no sympathy when he'd put himself in a compromising position and, according to Bill, had let his one-eyed monster do the thinking. His anger turned to pleading and his now ex-boss eventually hung up.

During the long lonely drive back to London, Grant wondered what to tell Catherine. He wanted them to grow old and grey together and knew he'd have to give her a reason for his job loss. He imagined she'd stand by him and support him as he tried to clear his name, and convince the powers that be he'd been set-up. Perhaps she could even help him uncover the truth about the establishment that was posing as a secure psychiatric facility. He felt better as he imagined them crusading together, their relationship becoming stronger by the day. Grant was totally in denial as the miles flew by until his phone pinged, indicating a new email. He pulled over at the earliest opportunity. Her message was short and sweet. He couldn't hide from the reality of the situation any longer and his false optimism disappeared as he read.

You bastard! Pack your stuff and be gone by the time I get home tomorrow. I never want to see you again. Beneath the text there was a photograph that showed Grant in all his glory and two women. Svetlana was astride him and the other…

'Oh shit,' he said out loud. He knew the only thing he was guilty of was temptation, but every picture told a story and there was no way he would be believed. His career was over and so was his relationship. He cut the engine and cried his heart out.

*****

Tony made his way to the buffet carriage ostensibly to buy coffees but also for a leg stretch and something to do. He noticed the woman who'd been on the platform and she quickly lifted a newspaper and hid behind it. If it hadn't been for the red hair and large sunglasses… when it clicked he carried on his way and was impatient to get the coffees and pass the information to Jim. Her curiosity had obviously got the better of her but it was important to avoid a confrontation. He would have to explain why they were on the Inverness train when they'd told their wives the training was in Manchester.

'That was quick,' said Jim and his tone changed when he saw the look on his brother's face.

'Oh Christ. What's happened now?'

'We're being followed.'

'Not dad again?'

Their father had already suspected they were special agents and had followed them when they intended to apprehend Big Ed.

'Nope.'

Jim could see Tony was enjoying himself, so played along.

'Mum, and she's brought some sandwiches.'

'Nope.'

'Must be Libby then.'

'Close and getting a lot warmer.' His humour had left him and Jim stopped laughing.

126

'You can't mean Fiona, surely?' But something clicked and he knew it was Fiona as soon as the words were out.

'But why and where and how did she know where we were.'

'She's the one I saw at the station. Heavily disguised but there was something about the way she moved that struck a chord. She tried to hide behind a newspaper when I went for the drinks and I didn't let on that I recognised her. That took some doing, I can tell you.'

Jim was thoughtful. On the one hand he knew he couldn't approach his wife without having to give her some explanation about why they were going to Inverness, on the other he was bloody furious she didn't trust him and had resorted to following them both.

'I've got a good mind to go and have it out with her. She knows how I feel about her, how dare she not trust me.'

Tony explained that, actually, Fiona had good reason not to trust her husband because he had in fact lied to her. 'I know, I know, even though it was in the interest of national security,' Tony pre-empted Jim's protest. 'But she does have a point.'

Jim grudgingly agreed. 'So. We can't talk to her and we can't lead her to the school either.' They were both thoughtful, trying to figure out the best way forward.

'We could use our evasion techniques but then she would know we're onto her.' It was a tricky situation so they decided to call the school.

After explaining to Janine they were told to remain on the train and await further instructions.

Janine hung up then hurried to the Director's office. She'd called ahead and Professor Robert reached the door at the same time. Violet was already inside and she pulled a blue folder out of her bag.

There was no small talk as they got straight down to business.

Violet passed the folder to the professor, pointing to the report she wanted him to read.

'Fiona called the company before the twins started their training and was very inquisitive.'

Robert listened as he quickly read the summary of the conversation.

'The operative said she was the most persistent and persuasive he'd ever had to deal with. When they hung up, he was convinced she hadn't believed him.'

The Director nodded, remembering when Violet had told him about Fiona.

'Why wasn't I informed?' The professor closed the file as he addressed his question to the Director. Seeing the expression on Janine's face the Director knew she was also unhappy at not being privy to the information.

'We would have told you both, and Ryan, if Mrs Sylvester had persisted. But nothing else happened and we believed she must have accepted... I know, I know,' he said as the professor was about to interrupt. 'I made the wrong call and I apologise.'

Not many bosses were willing to openly admit mistakes and apologise for them. The professor and Janine liked but also respected the Director and Violet hid her smile at her husband's apology, wondering why he was never as quick to apologise at home when he was in the wrong.

'What's the plan?' asked Janine.

'I suggest we bring her onside,' said Violet.

The professor and Janine were surprised but they could see the Director wasn't. 'Has this already been decided?'

'No, Robert. But I know how Violet's mind works.'

Robert allowed himself a smirk. They didn't discuss their personal relationship at work but there was bound to be the occasional crossover, and it was only natural they'd discuss the job at home.

'Katy's marrying her Marine and wants to leave so I need a new assistant. Fiona is intelligent, inquisitive and intuitive, not to mention single-minded and stubborn. I would much rather have her with us…' She let them think about the alternative, which would involve planning elaborate scenarios, and lies that Fiona would undoubtedly question.

'I would prefer to put our resources to good work against our enemies and not the partners of our operatives.'

It was Violet who returned the call.

'Do you think Fiona would like to work for us, Jim?'

When he recovered from his surprise Jim gave it some thought and Violet explained what she had in mind. 'I'll get back to you in a while.'

She knew he'd wish to discuss it with his brother so hung up and waited patiently.

'I can't understand why they'd offer her a job,' said Jim.

For a guy who was so bright, Tony thought his brother could be incredibly stupid at times. 'Okay, so do you want me to spell it out?' he didn't wait for an answer. 'She's nosey. She's like a dog with a bone once she gets an idea in her head. And she's one of the most stubborn and persistent people I've ever met.'

'Charming!'

'But she's also clever, intuitive, bright, practical, charismatic and great at reading body language.'

Jim felt better after this last bit.

'Put all that together with the fact she likes adventure and is bored in her current job and I should think she'd be the ideal candidate for a job at the school.'

'Well, when you put it like that, it's a no brainer.' So he wasn't the only one who thought his wife was special. It was his job to protect her and he wondered if this proposed role would put her in any danger. He came to the conclusion that it wouldn't and knew it would be better to have her with them. Like Tony said, she was clever and if she already knew he'd lied to her, what would she be like when they were on missions.

He called Violet and she told him how to proceed.

Fiona was absolutely fuming they were going to Inverness. Jim had lied about the location and she now knew he'd lied about the job. So what were they doing? She'd struggled to contain her anger initially but now she'd had time to think about it, she concluded that Jim and his brother would only lie to their wives to protect them. After she'd had that close call where she thought Tony had recognised her, she calmed her nerves and settled down. She spent the remainder of the journey wondering why the twins would want to protect their wives from what they were doing. Her assumptions were, she thought, far fetched but could they be plausible? She knew her husband too well to believe there was another woman involved and she also knew Tony adored Libby. So this was purely a work thing and Fiona recalled Graham telling her and Libby that the twins were special agents. She'd thought it was because he was a bit drunk at the time, but could there be any truth in it? She was still mulling it over as the train pulled into the station and she grabbed her bag and stepped onto the platform. Scanning the platform she couldn't see Jim or Tony, so making sure her collar was turned up and donning her clear glasses, she made her way to the exit, trying, but failing to go unnoticed.

'Hello, darling.' Fiona nearly jumped out of her skin. The twins had appeared directly in front of her, seemingly out of nowhere. 'What brings you to Inverness?' said Jim, purposely ignoring the warning signs that his wife was about to erupt.

'What brings me to Inverness, what brings me to…' she took a deep breath and closed her eyes. She didn't intend to have a major meltdown for all to see in Inverness Railway Station.

'Never mind what brings me here,' she hissed. 'What are you doing here? It's a long way from Manchester.'

'I received a call just after we left this morning,' said Tony. 'Asking if we could change our plans and visit the northern office at short notice, so here we are.'

To avoid a scene at the station, Violet had instructed Jim to lie to Fiona and she would be told the truth on arrival at the school.

'Our car's waiting. Come on, let's go.' Jim attempted to grab his wife's hand but she pulled away. She wasn't stupid and smelled a rat.

'Go where?'

'To work, Fi. Where else?'

He was being very evasive but it was either go with them or be stranded at the station so she chose the former, and they made their way to the car. A cold wind battered them as they hurried out of the station and Ryan opened the car door and greeted them warmly and quickly. He indicated that Fiona should sit up front then introduced himself properly when they were comfortably settled and the car heating on. Fiona warmed to him immediately and they all made small talk for a little while. Despite the convivial atmosphere she had an ever-increasing feeling that she was the only one in the car not privy to a secret. Half an hour passed and they seemed to be in the middle of nowhere. She couldn't stand it any more and turned around to face her husband and brother-in-law.

'Right you two. What's going on?'

'Now's not the place, Fi. All will become clear… later.'

'I need to know now, Jim. Why are you really here?'

'Why are you here, Fiona? Did you follow us?'

'Don't try and evade the question by turning it around to me, James Sylvester,' she raised her voice. 'Tell me now!'

'All right, all right.' Ryan's voice shook Fiona into silence. 'They haven't been working in Manchester, they've been training at a special school which is…'

'I was speaking to my husband if you don't mind.' Fiona interrupted then turned back to look at Jim.

'Fiona,' Ryan delivered the word with a no-nonsense tone of voice and Fiona turned back to face him. 'Please let me explain, it'll be easier.'

Her heartbeat quickened and she nodded, wary about the explanation that was to follow.

They were the only ones driving along the roads in the solitary part of the Highlands and Ryan judged it would be better to keep going rather than risk Fiona leaving the car if he stopped while he told her the truth. He didn't want to lock the door and make her even more anxious.

'Jim and Tony are training to be agents for a secret government agency.'

'And I'm the next Pope,' muttered Fiona. But even as she said it she knew there was a ring of truth in his statement. Jim's lies had been for a valid reason and her initial annoyance now turned to relief.

Ryan drove on in silence. He could see Fiona deep in thought but was surprised she hadn't had a go at her husband. She was a cool one.

'So your father was right all along?'

'No, sweetheart. We let dad think that because we couldn't explain the messages from Claire.'

'Why can't you tell your parents about Claire?'

'Because she's told us not to,' was Tony's simple reply.

'Doesn't it occur to you to ask why?'

'It doesn't work like that, Fi,' Jim sighed. 'Imagine we told Mum and Dad and then Claire speaks to us but not them. How do you think that would make them feel? Also, it's quite unusual...'

'No shit?'

'It's quite unusual and we don't want to be thought of as freaks. If we can do some good with Claire's help, that suits us.'

'So Claire's involved in all this?' Fiona swung her arms around, not sure what the *all this* was.

'We *heard* about the twins' special relationship with their sister when Big Ed Walton was caught, Fiona. We want to utilise this relationship along with their other talents, to help us in the fight against our enemies.'

'Oh shit.' Fiona had a random thought that she should find a more original expletive. After giving herself a mental telling off she returned to the matter at hand and thought about their new job. She had conveniently ignored the fact that it could be very dangerous and now it was starting to sink in. Jim noticed her change of expression.

'That's one of the reasons I didn't want you to know, Fi. To stop you from worrying.'

'Ignorance is bliss eh?' she shook her head. 'Did you really think you could keep it from me? And what about Libby?'

'Libby doesn't need to know.'

'Tony's right,' said Ryan. 'It's a lot to take in, Fiona but can I suggest that we all get to the school and have a good night's sleep. We'll explain everything in detail in the morning.'

Fiona nodded agreement but wondered why they'd told her if Libby was to be kept in the dark. She was tired but knew she was safe in the company of her husband and brother-in-law. She doubted she'd sleep much. Normally a very logical person, her thoughts were currently random and disorganised – like drivers in the centre of Paris – and she couldn't yet make sense of everything she'd been told. She'd keep quiet for now, get her head back in order, and prepare to find out further information the following day.

'Okay.'

Jim leaned forward and put a reassuring hand on his wife's shoulder. She squeezed it and he hoped that was a sign she'd forgive his deceit.

Chapter 14

Marion had said goodbye to Val and had packed her bag in the car.

'Are you sure you'll be able to cope without me?'

Libby could see the worry lines on her mother-in-law's face. She'd done so much for her mother and Libby would be forever grateful. She felt guilty because she wasn't looking forward to being on her own with her mother for four days, especially as the dreams had returned. The new tablets should have started to work by now but they hadn't noticed any changes.

'We'll be fine, Marion, honestly. You go and enjoy your reunion in Yorkshire. I hope it's not too cold up there. If there's no change we'll speak to the psychiatrist again when you get back.'

Marion mumbled her thanks and tried not to mention Yorkshire. She also tried to ignore the excitement that fizzed in her stomach anytime *the psychiatrist* was mentioned. It was early days in their relationship and she wanted to keep it all to herself for now. Letting her daughter-in-law believe she was going to a reunion was the best option. She hadn't exactly lied she said to herself, so there was no need to feel guilty. She drove off and less than an hour later parked her car in the garage that Basil had rented. She knocked on the door and the woman who answered made a record of the mileage and put the keys in an envelope. As agreed, Marion would pay when she collected the car on Monday afternoon. She caught a bus to the station shortly after then the train to the city. After initially trying to deny her feelings, she was now looking forward to spending a long weekend with the man she'd met through Val's unfortunate illness.

*****

Fiona was surprised when told she wouldn't be sharing a room with her husband and was shown to her own quarters. The room was comfortable and it reminded her of the better class hotel rooms she'd stayed in. She managed to get some sleep but had woken early, keen to discover more about the twins' role and the part she was to play. She wasn't stupid and had worked out she was to be involved in some capacity. Before eventually falling asleep she'd come to the conclusion she was to be offered a job. Her phone bleeped and Jim asked if she was ready for breakfast. When he knocked on her door a few minutes later she was surprised to hear that they'd already been for a run. No wonder his body was so toned. She shook her head as she remembered believing his story about training instead of going down the pub at night.

'What else have you lied about?' Was the morning greeting that Fiona gave her husband and he realised he'd been overly optimistic the previous night when he'd thought she'd forgiven him.

'Nothing, sweetheart, honestly.'

'Don't you *sweetheart* me, James Sylvester.' Fiona's hands were on her hips and he knew by her expression, and the fact that she'd used his full name, that he was in trouble.

'I'm really sorry but I didn't want to worry you and also we've signed the Official Secrets Act, Fi. If we disclose any information we could go to jail.'

She could see he was really worried and heard the pleading in his voice as he explained. The anger left her as quickly as it had arrived. So her husband was a trainee spy. And people thought James Bond was sexy?

Jim noticed the new look on Fiona's face and knew if he didn't tell her about the cameras he would be in real trouble with her later. He pulled her close to him and nuzzled her ear.

'I am genuinely sorry, Fi.'

'I know, you said.' She closed her eyes, enjoying the closeness of him, and moved to kiss him. Jim leaned back.

'I'm really sorry but when we arrived here there were CCTVs monitoring our rooms.' He would love nothing better than to spend a few hours in bed with his wife, but he certainly wasn't into performing in front of an audience.

'Ah,' Fiona broke their embrace. 'Breakfast it is then.'

She grabbed her bag from her room and closed the door. As they made their way to the mess hall Fiona wondered what other surprises were in store for her.

*****

Marion couldn't remember exactly how long it had been since she'd slept with a man. The last had been her ex, Graham, some years before. Even then she'd just gone through the motions, knowing they no longer loved each other but neither willing or ready to admit it. It had seemed like another lifetime away; before Claire's death and before she'd discovered her husband was living a double life. She was understandably nervous about making love with Basil but needn't have worried.

She was shaking when she removed her jacket. Although dressed in blouse and trousers, she felt naked when he looked at her. She'd looked after her body and was reasonably toned and fit, but Marion knew she didn't have the flawless perfection of a twenty-something. They kissed and he caressed her with his words as well as his lips.

'Don't be afraid, Marion. You're beautiful.'

She laughed nervously at first but by the time he'd removed her blouse and bra and his tongue and teeth teased her nipples, she was lost in the moment and forgot her earlier body shyness.

It had been so easy at first and then totally explosive. When he stroked her afterwards his touch seemed so natural. Now, as they lay in bed together on a Friday afternoon, it was as if she'd been awakened from a long sleep. She felt alive and it seemed that her black and white world had suddenly turned into glorious Technicolor. Everything looked more vibrant and all her senses were heightened. The noise from the wind and rain outside made her feel happy, cozied up inside with the man she loved. She remembered the first time she'd seen him - she knew then that if she fell, it would be hard and fast. When she got over the surprise that she did actually love this man Marion turned to look at him. His body was still lean despite his middle age. His face was peaceful and she looked at it in wonder, amazed she'd found someone who shared her sense of humour and who she could chat to about everything and nothing. His eyes opened and he smiled, making her feel like a teenager.

'Are you all right, Marion?'

She nodded in response and he held out his hand, which she enfolded in her own. He lifted hers to his lips and studied it as if it were the finest porcelain. He kissed it delicately then raised his eyes to hers, his face a picture of contentment.

'You aren't seeing anyone else, are you?' she'd explained how Graham had deceived her and Basil was totally understanding. His expression turned serious.

'No, I'm not. You can trust me and I'll do everything in my power not to hurt you. I'd like to tell my daughters about you and I'd like to meet your family, but only when you're ready.'

She knew he wouldn't push her and his patience and understanding were two other characteristics she loved about him. He'd told her he was in this for the long haul and had already declared his love. She felt totally comfortable in bed with this man as she laid her head on his chest. His fingers played delicate circles on her back and she started nuzzling his skin.

'I love you, Basil.'

He knew what it had taken for her to say those words and he couldn't remember how long it had been since he'd felt this happy.

'I'm so glad because I'd hate to think you were using me for my body.'

She grabbed his waist and tickled him. When he stopped giggling he kissed her with renewed passion. They made love with less urgency this time and Marion let him transport her to heaven and back.

*****

Libby was desperate for Marion to come home. Her mother was frantic and seemed to be convinced the man from her nightmares was coming to get her.

'They're dreams, Mum. He's dead. He can't hurt you any more.'

She'd been unable to convince her and now she was anxious and worried about her mother's sanity. It was nine o'clock in the morning and her mother was exhausted. She slept better during the day when the nightmares generally stayed away. Libby stroked her mother's head making soothing noises as if she were a child. Once Val nodded off she closed the bedroom door quietly. The ringing phone made her jump and she ran down the stairs to answer it, though there was little chance that it would wake her mother.

'Can I speak to Auntie Marion?'

'Hello, Mel. How are you?'

There was silence on the other end of the phone and Libby repeated the question, not sure if the line had gone dead.

'I'm a bit scared, Libby. I need to speak to Auntie Marion please.'

There must be something in the air today thought Libby. 'Auntie Marion's away and won't be back until later on... Mel, what is it?' Libby could hear the gentle sobs on the other end of the phone.

'I, I...'

'All right, Mel. Take your time... I'll help you if I can. What is it?'

Silence again, as the teenager tried to compose herself. 'I've had nightmares for the last three nights. The awful man who kidnapped me appeared...'

Libby could hear the panic in her voice.

'He said he was coming to get me and this time he'd kill me...'

Libby paled.

'I'm scared, Libby. Really scared.'

'Okay, Mel. You know that he's dead don't you?'

'Yes,' she replied between gulps, trying to regain control thought Libby.

'And you know that dead people can't hurt you don't you?'

'I know, Libby but it was like, so real. I've never had such vivid dreams before.'

'What did your parents say, Mel?'

'Dad went to Portugal last night for one of his competitions and Mum's going to join him in a few days. I didn't want to worry them and I'm coming to stay with you guys again, so...'

Libby knew the notorious Big Ed was the same man who had kidnapped Mel and duped her mother, so it was logical they would both have flashbacks and bad memories from their association with him. It still seemed more than coincidence that their nightmares were at the same time. She shivered involuntarily when thinking about it. She forced herself back to reality having no desire to spook Mel further.

'Auntie Marion will be back this afternoon so I'll ask her to call you. In the meantime I think you should tell your Mum, she's bound to notice you're upset about something and will only worry if you don't.'

Mel said she would talk to her mother but Libby wasn't convinced. They hung up and as Libby pondered the conversation, she decided to call Marion who would be on her way back from Yorkshire by now.

*****

The weekend had flown by and they were both sad when it was time to say goodbye on Monday morning.

'When Val's a bit better and the boys are home from whatever course they're doing I'll tell them all.'

'There's never going to be an ideal time, Marion.'

'I know, I know but I want all the teasing over in one and that means with Libby and Fiona as well. But God only knows where Fiona is at the moment, she's more independent than me that one.'

They laughed but Basil was well aware this was Marion's feeble attempt at changing the subject.

'Look, we love each other and I want to show you off. What are you afraid of?'

She hugged him and wished she could answer his question. 'I really don't know. You're the psychiatrist, you tell me.'

Marion's phone interrupted their conversation.

'Hi, Libby. Yes I can talk. I've stopped at the Services for a coffee.' She looked at Basil and crossed her fingers uncomfortable about lying to her daughter-in-law. As she listened quietly he noticed the look of concern on her face.

'Yes, you did the right thing. I think she should tell her mother too. Carol will be worried about her

141

and I'm not comfortable with her staying with us if Carol doesn't know what's going on...'

The conversation continued. It seemed one sided to Basil with Marion answering *yes* or *uh huh* occasionally. His ears perked up when she had more to say.

'Okay. He's back in this afternoon is he? We'll try to contact him when I get home and ask his advice. Or depending on my timing, I might call him before I get back,' she grimaced while telling another lie. 'We should try and convince your mother to have another appointment so he can assess her properly.'

Marion knew Libby must be very worried. Thankfully, she hadn't asked about her weekend. That was the only thing she was relieved about when they finished the call.

Basil waited patiently for her to gather her thoughts, further conversation about outing their relationship put on the back burner for the time being.

'Val's having dreams again, about Gary.' Her expression changed when she said his name and Basil knew she despised the man, although he was dead, for what he'd done to her friend and to her surrogate niece, Melanie. 'Libby says the tablets aren't working and if anything she's getting worse... I wonder if it's because I'm not there. Perhaps I shouldn't have left her?' she didn't wait for him to reply. 'Mel's having nightmares about the same man too. What the hell's going on? He's dead and he's still bothering them... Will that man always haunt them? Even though he's dead, he's still in all our lives...'

Basil remained silent until Marion was spent.

'Val first, and I'd tell you this anyway so I'm not breaking professional etiquette. I'd like to see her again, ideally as an in-patient. She's not a danger to herself or anyone else so I can't section her, Marion, only advise.' He avoided adding that she wasn't a danger to herself *yet* to avoid worrying Marion further, and hoped that timely intervention would mean Val would improve. But he was the first to admit that some people never recovered and could suffer from depression for life.

'I know that, but it's so frustrating. Sometimes I don't think she wants to be helped.'

'I know, I know,' he held her hand. 'You're the best friend she could ask for and you're doing everything you can and so is Libby. Try and get her to come to see me and I'll do what I can too.'

Easier said than done thought Marion but she would double her efforts and if she sat down with Val while Libby was there as well, maybe they could talk her into it.

As for Melanie,' Basil continued. 'It's understandable she has the odd nightmare. She went through a terrifying experience that's going to stay with her forever.'

Marion wondered whether to tell him about the feeling she'd experienced, that an evil presence was in her house. She decided against it knowing imagination could play tricks during the dark hours that seemed ludicrous in the cold light of day.

'What is it?' he was totally tuned into her and Marion was impressed.

'Nothing.'

Basil wasn't convinced but he didn't push it.

'Might Mel have overheard a conversation about Val's nightmares when she was staying with you?'

'Of course,' Marion clicked her fingers. 'You know Val spends most of the time in her room and Libby and I often discuss what's going on. I didn't even consider it might affect Mel...' she shook her head and frowned. 'How totally insensitive of me.'

'Don't be hard on yourself, Marion. You're a wonderful woman who always thinks of others. It's time to put yourself first.'

'What do you think I've been doing this weekend,' she winked and nudged him in the waist and the mood lightened.

'You've made me feel better, Basil. But you always do.'

He pulled her toward him and they shared one last, lingering kiss. Thoughts of everyone else disappeared as they savoured the moment.

Chapter 15

Big Ed knew Val was getting weaker every time he visited. Initially disappointed, his ego was bruised by her rejection, and as he saw it, denial of her feelings for him. He was determined to make her see sense. He felt himself becoming stronger with the passing of time and knew to make his plan work he would need to up the ante. He was also happy to scare the girl Mel but was merely using her to relieve his occasional boredom. The only serious plans he had were for Val. Ignoring the caution from his useless father, he decided to test his abilities and searched for a target. It wasn't long before he found his first prey.

Barry was a victim of alcohol and the recession. His wife had left him and he couldn't remember whether the alcohol had come first or the loss of his business. According to his ex, the alcohol had caused his downfall and not the recession. It made no difference now. Barry had joined the other down and outs in the city. The first thing he reached for when he woke up was a bottle and when he did sleep, it was never far from his side.

Barry had fallen asleep in the park bushes and the warden had missed him on his final check before locking the gates. There were many places for people to hide in the park so he didn't always find those who didn't want to be found, before closing for the night. Even in his drunken stupor the sharp edges of the bush woke Barry. He staggered to the nearest bench and curled up on it, covering himself with his dirty old blanket, then held his bottle as if it were a lover he didn't want to let go.

Big Ed forced his way into Barry's body and mind as he slept on the bench. Barry woke following a strange dream about a long journey on a boat with a lot of young girls. He moved to unscrew the top off his bottle, his usual morning habit, and was frustrated when he was unable to do so.

'Not today, my friend,' said a voice and Barry tapped the side of his head with his palm, wondering what was happening. He was sober and something wasn't right. He needed a drink.

'I said not today.' The voice sounded angry this time. Barry watched as his own hand raised the bottle level with his head and he swung his arm behind him. He was powerless to stop himself from throwing the bottle away, and wailed as he saw it smashed into smithereens some distance in front of him. The voice in his head laughed and told him to get some breakfast. Barry staggered out of the park. It was still early and nobody was about to hear the argument between his own voice and the one that had invaded his thoughts.

The warden had opened the gates at six o'clock and the town was starting to come alive. As Big Ed looked through the eyes of the vagrant he saw people moving about and the traffic building up on the roads. Always a fit man in his human life he was disgusted at the way the vagrant had let himself go. He was wheezing after a short walk and it took all of Big Ed's strength to drag him away from every dustbin where he looked for cigarette butts and leftovers from the previous night's meals.

The possession was taking its toll on Big Ed; it was tiring and he was frustrated he didn't yet have the strength to gain total control of this weak individual. Consequently a number of busy commuters body swerved the mad tramp that was walking along the pavement arguing loudly with himself.

Big Ed used the last of his strength to smash the window of a fast food restaurant, steal the breakfast in a roll from right under the nose of a hungry patron, and run down the street with it. He managed to force Barry to eat half of the fatty food before exhaustion took over and he left the vagrant's body, conceding defeat. He looked down with satisfaction as he saw the annoyed patron had caught up with Barry and was giving him a good kicking for stealing his breakfast. *Serve the bastard's right* thought Big Ed before he found a place where he could rest and recharge. Totally beat his last thought was that the next body and mind he possessed would be better than the pathetic vagrant's.

*****

Fiona had enjoyed the tasty breakfast but not the conversation, which had seemed false and stilted. She looked forward to discovering more so she could talk to her husband and brother-in-law without the distinct impression they were keeping secrets from her.

'We have to get on,' said Jim. 'But we've been asked to take you to the conference room to meet some people.'

'Who?'

'Violet and Janine. Violet recruited us and Janine works here.'

Fiona still wasn't sure what exactly went on *here* but followed the twins, eager for the puzzle to be pieced together.

Shortly after they arrived at the conference room Jim and Tony disappeared following the introductions.

'Coffee?' asked Janine and Fiona declined. 'I've just had breakfast thanks.'

'I have a proposition for you, Fiona,' said Violet. 'Would you like me to explain or would you prefer we answer your questions first?' Violet knew very well what her answer would be.

'I'm intrigued. Please explain.'

'I believe Jim has already mentioned that I recruited them?' Fiona nodded. 'My assistant is leaving and I have a vacancy. I wondered if you'd be interested?'

So there really was a job offer. Fiona tried to hide her surprise. 'I think I will have a coffee actually.' She was stalling while she thought about whether she'd want a job that could involve recruiting spies. Not one to beat around the bush, Fiona couldn't contain her excitement any longer.

'Hell, yes.'

'But you don't know what the job involves yet?'

'Does it involve recruiting spies?'

Violet and Janine laughed. They found Fiona's obvious enthusiasm and honesty refreshing, but Violet also knew she'd have to learn to curb those traits. 'It certainly does.'

'When can I start?'

Now that she had initially accepted the offer, she was given further details of the position. Fiona was disappointed to hear she'd have to serve something of an apprenticeship before she could be let loose on her own initiative. No matter, she hadn't felt this enthusiastic since she'd started her first job and was looking forward to her training. She was surprised to hear that background checks on her family and friends had already taken place. Violet explained they hadn't found any skeletons in the closet and that the first part of her training would involve an overview of the organisation and basic security principles. This part of the training would take place down south and they discussed a credible cover story for Fiona to tell those she needed to.

'Does anyone else know that you suspected Jim and Tony were up to something?' asked Violet. 'We need to cover your tracks.'

'I didn't mention it to Libby because she's too busy with her mother and I didn't want to worry her about anything else.'

'Well that's good news. It means...'

'Actually. I talk to my friend Kayleigh about everything but she knows me too well to know when I'm keeping something from her. So that could be difficult.' Fiona caught the look that passed between the two women.

'Or not as the case might be,' she muttered as her brain worked overtime. 'You're not telling me that Kayleigh...' Fiona shook her head, incredulous even though her suspicions were not yet confirmed.

'Very perceptive, Fiona. Kayleigh does work for us but in a different department.'

'But we've been friends for years.'

'Yes. So you know how much Kayleigh values your friendship. It was useful that we could obtain information from her. She's a professional but really worried that she's jeopardised your friendship. I know she's going to be delighted once she discovers you've accepted the job. When you realise we lie to our family and friends to protect them and in the interests of national security, I'm sure you'll be able to forgive Kayleigh.'

Fiona contemplated the information. *National Security* seemed to be the umbrella they used to justify their deceit and she wasn't yet sure how she felt about that. Her husband and brother-in-law had lied to her and the rest of the family, and her best friend was also some sort of agent. She needed further clarification before moving forward.

'Any more surprises? I mean, any other members of my family involved, or friends, work colleagues?'

'One member of your netball club does some ad hoc work for us, Fiona. She helps us as and when we need it.'

Fiona wracked her brains trying to work out who it might be. 'Trudy! It has to be. She's away retraining at the moment. It's got to be Trudy.' Fiona felt a little smug. 'And you're positive that's it, nobody else?'

'As I said, Fiona. Just the one member of your netball club and I don't want you to discuss your work with her.'

'Okay.'

'Now, are you ready for further details and a tour of the school?'

Fiona said she was. Violet decided not to tell her she was wrong, but to see how long it would take her to work out the real identity of the agent. She wouldn't play netball for a while so would discover the truth before she next spoke to Trudy.

*****

While Fiona was being apprised of the situation, the twins were about to receive a briefing on their first mission. The Director wanted their first to be a relatively simple one so he could assess them whilst under pressure. If they overcame the obstacles he was sure they would find and if he remained confident in their abilities, they'd be sent to tackle bigger and more urgent problems.

'Somebody with inside information has been in contact with the press,' said Ryan. 'The Director wants to know who and why. We have our suspicions.' He explained that Isobel was a disgruntled employee who felt she'd been passed over for promotion. 'We've already taken measures to limit her information on current operations but she still knows too much.'

'You want us to catch her at it?' asked Tony.

'We want you to monitor her movements when she's not in work. We know there's no point monitoring her calls because she's not stupid enough to use her own phone, or computer come to that. She must have contacted Grant Chatham from a public phone or Internet Cafe so we need to know where.'

150

'I assume you need enough information to be able to sack her?'

'Sack and maybe even prosecute, Jim. At the very least we need her out of the organisation, but even we can't get rid of someone just because we suspect them of whistleblowing. We must have incriminating evidence.'

They discussed various ways to proceed with the surveillance and Ryan became a little uncomfortable.

'Right. You know my feelings on all of this but I've been told to ask you if you can err... ask for help...'

'You mean Claire?'

'Yes, your sister.' Although he'd heard the evidence for himself, Ryan still felt uneasy about discussing their relationship with their dead sister and it showed.

'We can ask, Ryan,' said Tony. 'But she hasn't been around for a little while so there's no guarantee she will assist.'

'Sorry but we might just have to go this one alone,' added Jim.

Chapter 16

Claire opened her eyes. She felt refreshed and ready for action. She ran her fingers down Raphael's sleeping face in the hope he would wake. There wasn't even a flicker and she started to wonder if he would ever return to her.

Leaving him she tried to focus on the present. Feeling apprehensive she knew she was strong and that her talents were expanding. She was also acutely aware that if her plan didn't succeed, chaos would reign on Earth resulting in many more innocent people being slaughtered before their time. A large number of the new spirits she'd already met had died too soon. This was all due to the overpowering presence of too many evils and she was determined to do what she could to redress the balance. She hoped some of the newbies would have the opportunity for another life but that was for others to decide. Claire focused all her energy on the current phase of the operation. She gave herself a good talking to trying to boost her confidence and ego. If she failed it would be her own doing and they'd take her to Hell. Still feeling guilty about the eighteen new spirits who had already been lost to the demons, Claire decided to go it alone.

She was able to gravitate to where trouble was kicking off and she looked at the scene below her. It was that mysterious twilight time of day and a woman was pushing a pushchair, the child inside sleeping soundly. A gang of youths appeared and one of them started talking to the woman. Claire couldn't hear what was being said but could see the woman looked nervous. Every time she tried to wheel the pushchair around the youths, one of them blocked her way. The woman now looked terrified and the small gang were using her as sport, laughing and taunting as she tried to make her way out of the park before darkness descended. Claire zoomed down into the park and targeted the ringleader. It took very little effort on her part to trip him and he landed on his butt.

'What the...'

A few of his mates laughed. 'Enjoy your trip, Andy?'

Andy got to his feet, not amused.

'Think it's fucking funny do you, Rick?' He swaggered over to Rick and started pushing and prodding him.

The woman was surprised the ringleader had appeared to trip over nothing, but soon sprang into action. She took advantage of the diversion and rushed off, putting as much distance between herself and the yobs as she could. She knew she wouldn't use the park as a short cut in the future unless accompanied by other adults.

The evils had seen Claire but were too busy enjoying themselves to take much notice of her. They were either very confident or stupid she thought as she centred herself ready to ruin their eternity. The first two didn't know what hit them as she drew them into her aura of love and kindness. Her thoughts and feelings were anathema to the evils and although they screamed with fury, she was far too powerful. She visualised the hated cockroach form and watched as the dark light of one of the evils initially turned into its former human self. She was surprised he had a gentle-looking face; it always amazed her that even lovely faces could hide immense evil. The eyes normally gave it away though and true to form, the eyes of this middle-aged man were brown pools of cruelty. No matter. She concentrated and was rewarded as his human form transmuted from the feet up. He looked down at his body and watched from his human eyes as his body mutated into that of a cockroach. The screaming stopped once the transformation was

153

complete. Claire wrapped him in a force field and watched as the cockroach head butted the invisible barrier, trying unsuccessfully to escape. The second followed quickly and Claire looked around.

'Two down, about thirty to go,' she said to herself and rubbed her hands together in a business-like fashion. There was some resistance and some fought back. None were able to put a dent in Claire's strength and she soon had her catch of thirty-two. She knew it was only a small victory but reminded herself that success could very well depend on the repetition of small efforts. During the gathering Claire hadn't had time to think about how she'd achieved her first successes. Now that she did she was pleasantly surprised her talents were still expanding and she seemed able to accomplish anything she put her mind to. Satisfied, she sped off toward the cave taking her *bag* of evil, angry cockroaches with her.

Not much later she delivered her prize and was surprised to discover Ron and Sandy were now on bat duty.

'Who authorised this?'

'Zach received orders from the Committee, Claire.' Ron knew Claire wouldn't get stroppy if she was told the orders came from the highest level.

She looked around her. As well as Ron and Sandy, other reinforcements had arrived and they all seemed to be working well together, containing the many newly delivered evils. Ron pre-empted her next question.

'Don't ask me how but the Committee have heard about your plan. They've organised other angels so you're not the only one gathering evils.'

'How many?'

'We've met five new angels, Claire,' said Sandy. 'Not all of them are as strong as you, but the ones that aren't are working together and so far none have been taken.'

That was a relief. Claire didn't want the fate of others on her conscience.

'One told us the Committee will be sending more as and when they can but they're going to need more of us in the cave to contain them too,' said Ron. The way they ping-ponged the conversation reminded Claire of her brothers.

'Apparently some stronger and more senior angels will arrive soon. They'll be more capable of containing this lot and other new deliveries as the numbers increase.' Sandy informed Claire and she couldn't fault the logic of the Committee. They would definitely need strong characters in the cave to avoid a repetition of their current situation. Confident that all was well there, Claire said her goodbyes and made her was back to Cherussola to check in with Zach, and to see if there was any news of Raphael.

*****

Isobel had tried without success to get through to the editor of *The Investigator*. Deep down she acknowledged she wouldn't get anything from that newspaper and was fuming that the stupid journalist had allowed himself to be caught in a compromising position. She believed she could still make money out of her story but was growing impatient. Not looking forward to a boring career as an archivist she knew if she didn't act now, she never would. She'd done her homework and decided to try her luck with others. The first three wouldn't give her the time of day. An employee of the fourth, *The Enquirer* and major rival of Grant Chatham's old paper, wanted to meet with her.

Jim had grown a beard and moved into a bedsit down the street from Isobel's home. With his longer hair and thickly rimmed spectacles, he looked nothing like his usual self. The twins were still learning the art of make-up and prosthetics but Tony had done a good job on his nose, and even a professional who looked at him closely would have trouble distinguishing the real from the fake. Along with his wig and skin darkening cream his disguise was complete. He was dressed in nondescript clothing and walked with a slight hunch. He didn't warrant a second look from anyone he passed and when Jim called to tell him that Isobel was headed into town, he followed her without her noticing. There was only one Internet Cafe in the town and Tony made a call from outside after he watched Isobel enter. He was confident he could hack into the computers. They'd been trained in breaking and entering techniques but hadn't had the opportunity to put their training into practise. He arranged to meet Jim and they decided to contact Ryan for advice.

*****

'What O, everyone and welcome.'

Claire listened to Zach welcoming the latest newbie spirits. He sounded more like a posh holiday rep giving a new arrivals welcome speech to tourists, than an angel talking to the newly dead. She knew he was as mad as a sock full of frogs but still, he'd done a brilliant job so far. It wouldn't be much longer until the newbies would be turned into bats and despatched to the cave to help Ron and Sandy. As long as she could overcome the evils, turn them into cockroaches and get them into the cave there wasn't a problem. The bats already in the cave had felt a renewed sense of optimism on the arrival of Ron and Sandy, and when Claire had told them the plan. She was amazed at what a little hope could do. She couldn't deny there was a special aura about the cave and she was sure that helped their cause. Claire didn't waste further time trying to work out what was special about the place. Her job was to fight the fight and nothing would turn her from that task.

Knowing that eventually she would have to overcome major evils such as Big Ed meant that Claire had to start picking off the stronger and more important individuals. She was too wary to tackle the worst of them without back up, but had decided her next target should be the Goth with whom she'd had an earlier run-in. Claire set off to find her with single-minded determination.

*****

It was the first time in his adult life that Grant Chatham had been unemployed and he found it tough. He knew he was a good journalist but nobody would touch him with a bargepole after the incriminating photographs had gone public. He'd pleaded with Catherine to take him back in various answerphone messages but she wouldn't answer his calls. She'd even changed her number and he'd received a police warning for repeatedly contacting her. To make matters worse that bloody woman who'd started it all kept calling and hassling him. Sick of staring at the walls in the barren looking flat he'd rented, he made his way to the pub on the corner of the street.

The conversation with the bloke Tom had started amicably enough and Grant was cheered by the banter. Grant almost felt like an outside force was manipulating him and when Tom had laughed and told him that his team would go down at the end of the season, he totally lost it. As he wasn't a fighter or a violent man, the nature of his reaction would shock him to the core once the affects of the alcohol wore off.

Grant opened his eyes and looked around. He didn't recognise his surroundings at first and started to panic. His face felt strange. He touched it gingerly and grimaced. One side was much bigger than the other and he knew he'd have a black eye and possibly a fractured cheekbone. Grant put his head in his hands trying to make the world disappear. Now sober, the

157

events of the previous night returned. He managed to piece it all together. He'd thrown the first punch and recalled the surprised look on Tom's face. Tom told him to calm down and hadn't retaliated, initially. Grant punched him again – Tom's look of surprise turned to rage when he responded with gusto. Although he'd felt murderous Grant had picked up second place and spent the night in the cell.

'Morning, Rocky,' the policeman's voice shook him from his reverie.

'What did you call me?' Grant knew he had rights.

'I said good morning, Mr Chatham. How are you on this bright but cold day?' The door was unlocked and Grant accompanied the policeman to a reception area. There were a few vagrants there who looked as if they'd been happy to have a cell for the night and one other man whom two policemen were restraining. His belongings were returned to him before Grant signed papers informing him he was to appear in court at a time and date to be confirmed. He made his way home slowly, wondering how he'd allowed himself to get to this point in his life.

*****

The twins had wondered what Janine's special talents were for some time. There was nothing obvious so they assumed she was simply very clever and an extremely good instructor. Standing at the back of the Internet Cafe on that bitter Scottish night they were given a small insight into what else she could do. Donned in black and wearing balaclavas, they watched as Janine made breaking into the building look like child's play. As previously agreed, she'd disappeared as soon as her part in the mission was complete. They entered stealthily then Jim jumped onto a chair to disable the camera. After less than a minute he removed his balaclava and returned to floor level.

158

'It's one of the false ones, totally non-operational.'

'You sure?'

He gave Tony a look hastily scanning the area while his brother worked on the first computer. Crouched low Jim watched for movements on the high street. It was deadly quiet as there was nobody brave enough to venture out on the bitter night. Jim knew they couldn't be too complacent and kept a steady watch, leaving Tony to concentrate on his job of searching for any correspondence from Isobel. If he came up blank he would use state of the art technology to bug the computers and would monitor their traffic from his own machine using a series of different URLs. He was already a computer whizz kid and hadn't needed to attend many IT classes at the school.

He got lucky on the second computer, as Isobel hadn't deleted her browsing history. He found the emails she'd sent through the newspapers' own websites and he also discovered a positive response she'd received from one with a contact number and name. Tony made a note of the details and of Isobel's email address. He decided he would monitor the other computers anyway, in case she returned to correspond with her new contact. He was confident in his ability to evade discovery by any employees or visitors to the Internet Cafe. It always amazed Tony that people used these places without encrypting their personal details, yet were surprised when their accounts were hacked.

Surveillance was boring and the twins felt like pulling their hair out during the following days when Isobel went to work, came home, spent some time with her mother and her kids, followed by a bit of shopping. They struck lucky on the fourth day when she called in sick then made her way to the railway station. They followed her to London. Being a creature of habit Isobel carried out the same routine with the journalist from *The Enquirer* as she had with *The Investigator*. She didn't notice the forgettable man who was sitting in the cafe reading his newspaper and seemingly minding his own business. The evidence gathered as ordered, Jim called Ryan on the secure line.

'All done, Ryan and we have the incriminating evidence, all recorded. We should be back tomorrow.'

'Something's come up.' Ryan explained they were to stay put and await further instructions. 'We have another job for you. In the meantime get Tony to encrypt the evidence and email it to me here. I'll pass it to the Director who will deal with Isobel as he sees fit.' The call ended and the twins returned to their hotel to await further instructions.

*****

Libby flung open the front door before Marion had a chance to put her key in the lock. Her daughter-in-law flung her arms around her squeezing her tight.

'Good grief, you'd think I'd just been rescued from terrorists, not been away for three days.'

'Four, Marion. Four days and it's been absolute hell.'

'Don't be such a drama queen.' She followed Libby into the house, pleased to see the kettle already on.

'Right. Let's have a cuppa and you can tell me all about it.'

Marion felt totally different to how she had when she'd left her home on Friday. Everything looked sharper and brighter and she wasn't looking forward to getting back into the routine of caring for Val. She was sure she must look different but Libby hadn't noticed.

They sat down with their tea. Libby couldn't wait any longer.

'I'm so worried about my mother, Marion, and poor Mel too. What if there is a link? When can we call her doctor? What about Mel? Her family must be really worried.'

'Stop.'

Marion's raised voice silenced her. 'We know there is a link so it's understandable they've both had nightmares about that awful man. Luckily Mel made a good recovery, but his death, and the fact she probably heard our conversations about your mother's nightmares, could have brought it all back.'

'I'm sorry, I didn't think. I...'

'Neither of us did, Libby and I'm sorry too. Anyway, I've already spoken to Basil. He's the psychiatrist,' she explained when Libby looked confused. 'He's given your mother the maximum strength tablets he can without seeing her again.' She leaned toward her daughter-in-law to emphasise her next point. 'It's very important for your mother to have another appointment so he can reassess her condition. Depression can last for years so she needs to be monitored.'

'But that's the problem. Mum doesn't want to see anyone at the moment.'

'We can only help her further if she helps herself.'

'Marion!'

Marion hadn't meant to snap but her weekend away reminded her that she had her own life. Although she loved Val dearly she was getting tired of pandering to her every need and believed drastic action was now required.

'I'm sorry, Libby but perhaps if we employed shock tactics and your mother moved back to her own place she'd be forced to face reality and look after herself.' Marion didn't believe it even as she said the words, but was at a loss as to what to do next.

'Please don't throw her out, Marion. I don't know how she'd cope without you. Me neither.'

161

Libby started crying and Marion regretted her moment of selfishness. She held her, muttering words of comfort and telling her that her mother would get better but it would take time. They both knew she was only saying the words to make Libby feel better. When the tears subsided Marion said she'd see how Val was doing. She wasn't in the mood so was relieved her friend was sleeping.

'Can't she have therapy or treatment or something as an in-patient?' asked Libby when Marion returned.

She explained that as Val wasn't a danger to herself or anyone else she couldn't be forced to undergo treatment. 'We'll talk to her again tonight and try to get her to see some sense. In the meantime, I need to find out how Mel's getting on.'

After a long chat with Mel she managed to convince her to talk to her mother. A little while later Carol called to thank Marion for her intervention.

'We've decided that Mel's coming to Portugal with me after all. She'll give you a call to tell you all about it when we get home. How was your weekend by the way? Did you have a nice break?'

The immediate concerns about Mel having been dealt with, Marion gave some nondescript information about her weekend, ending the call with a relieved sigh. 'Well thank goodness for that,' she said to Libby, smiling. She would be sad not to see Mel – the teenager's company was a welcome relief from the arduous task of caring for Val – but at the same time she was glad Mel had confided in her mother and grateful that she had one less person to worry about.

*****

'Isobel, come with me please.' said Mr Smart. She looked up from her monitor in irritation. He was no longer her line manager and she told him so.

162

'This is a security matter, Isobel. Now please.' He opened the door waiting for her to follow. Standing up she pushed her chair under the desk. Seeing the look on his face forced her to readjust her attitude and she knew something was amiss. Guilty thoughts started running through her mind, even though she'd been extremely careful and had covered her tracks. They couldn't have found out, it must be something else.

'Where are we going?'

'Just follow me.'

Her heart started beating faster and she broke into a cold sweat, as she feared the worst.

They arrived at the Director's outer office and Isobel knew they'd found out. Shoulders slumped she followed Mr Smart. The efficient PA told him to go right in and Isobel to wait. She hadn't been told to take a seat but was too nervous anyway. The PA ignored her as she paced up and down the spacious area, awaiting her call. She didn't have long to wait. The PA's phone buzzed. Isobel was told to go on in.

'Good morning, Isobel.'

'Good morning, Director.' She was annoyed her voice sounded shaky.

'Do you know why I've called you here?'

She shook her head, not trusting herself to speak.

'Take a seat,' it was an order not a request and she did as told. 'Now listen to this.'

Mr Smart pressed a button. They all remained quiet as her voice and that of the journalist from *The Enquirer* filled the room. The Director and Mr Smart sipped their coffees as they watched Isobel disintegrate in front of them. Mr Smart increased the volume when the tears turned into loud sobs that wracked her whole body. The Director buzzed for his PA who entered the room to place a box of tissues on the table, before leaving discreetly. Silence followed when the recording finished and both men waited for her to regain her composure.

'I have two children to feed and clothe.'

'You should have thought of that before you broke the Official Secrets Act,' said Mr Smart. 'It's going to be difficult trying to feed them from your cell.'

The harsh words brought on more tears so the Director waited for her to stop crying.

'You're sacked, Isobel without any pension or gratuity, and like Mr Smart says, you could very well go to prison.'

He let the information sink in while noting the new ashen colour of her complexion.

'I'm sorry, I didn't meant it to happen like this. It wasn't...'

'Save it for the jury, Isobel, or the press. I imagine you'll try to sell your story when you come out. Your kids will likely be grown up by then. Who'll look after them? Your mother or your ex?'

It was the final comment that did it. He wasn't enjoying the interview and noted without pleasure they now had her where they wanted, so the rest should be quick and easy.

'Please. I can't go to prison. I'll do anything you want but don't make me go to prison.' She meant every word, knowing she'd run out of options.

The Director concluded the interview by dismissing Isobel. He knew he'd silenced her and that she wouldn't be any further threat to the organisation. He told Mr Smart she'd be relocated with her family and found a job in the supermarket where one of their agents was employed.

'I'm pretty sure she's no longer a threat but he can keep an eye on her, just in case.'

'With all due respect, sir, is that how we punish disloyalty?'

'Use your brain, Smarty. You know as well as I do that you can never trust people like Isobel one hundred per cent. She'll have enough to live a reasonable lifestyle without being tempted to blow the whistle again. And if she does...' he left the rest to Mr Smart's imagination. 'My immediate concern now is to put the press off the trail. Even though Isobel's going to tell her contact it was a mistake, he may still smell a rat,' he was thoughtful for a moment. 'I have an idea. Do you think with a little help, he'll discover her underlying mental health issues, and...' The Director smiled.

*****

The twins had changed their disguise so they looked alike but not identical. They told their new acquaintances they were brothers. They'd been quite loud in the pub, agreeing with the other men who all hated the fact their country was being taken over and their jobs stolen by foreigners. Tony and Jim could feel the evil in the atmosphere as their new mates worked themselves up into a frenzy, deciding they weren't going to accept the situation any longer. It was time for action. The demo was arranged for the following weekend. One of the men advised them on the best weapons to use when they came up against any opposition. Tony passed the details to Ryan who informed the police and arranged for their presence. He told Tony and Jim to be careful. They replied that he shouldn't worry. They'd provide the authorities with the names of the troublemakers if they weren't apprehended at the demo.

The atmosphere was charged on the day of the demo. The twins remembered the warning from their sister and wondered if evil forces were actually at work now. They looked around as the number of people gathering increased by the minute. Jackets and coats that normally looked flat were bulked out and uneven,

165

where the owners were unsuccessfully trying to hide their weapons. Some carried banners proclaiming messages such as: *England for the English* and *Give our jobs back*. The guys from the pub didn't even pretend they were interested in a peaceful demo, and the twins knew they were spoiling for a fight. A few scuffles broke out between the opposing demonstrators then one of their crowd lost his temper and started laying into a peaceful member of the opposition. Police with riot shields appeared. The man had the rage upon him and resisted arrest. He was overpowered and secured in one of the black police vans.

'How come so many fucking coppers?' asked one.

'We've been grassed up,' said another. Let's get out of here.' Realising they were outnumbered they started to leave. Tony and Jim were about to part company but were encouraged to go with them. Underestimating the intelligence of their new friends they didn't suspect they were in trouble. They all ran for a while, disappointed at the demo but still buoyed up by the small skirmishes and the fact they'd been able to inflict some pain on the opposition. They came to a disused building, obviously one of their hideouts thought the twins. The brothers felt a worrying change in the atmosphere when the other twelve blokes turned to them. One walked slowly tapping his baseball bat in his free hand as he did so. His intention was obvious.

'I think we're in a bit of trouble,' said Jim.

'No shit Sherlock,' replied Tony as the other men joined the first. The twins stood back to back as their enemy formed a circle around them.

Claire found the Goth. Appearing in her human form she was overseeing a number of minions. Claire noted with satisfaction that her minions were smaller in number than during their previous encounter. The Goth looked directly at Claire acknowledging her presence but seemingly unconcerned. Claire was miffed. The Goth obviously thought she wasn't a threat. How very dare she! Claire remembered why she was doing this and calmed herself. Ignoring the amassing crowds she concentrated her thoughts. When she felt ready she started picking off some of the Goth's assistants. Now in the right frame of mind, it was time to tackle madam herself. She approached with caution. The Goth turned to face her before Claire reached her. It was her toughest task so far and she spun around for a bit as the strength of the evil's kick took her by surprise. Claire returned, doubling her efforts. They paid off and she tried to hide her satisfaction at the look of horror on her enemy's face, as her feet and legs started to transmute. Claire had transformed the Goth's body; only the head of the grotesque creature was left. The Goth-roach stopped screaming and, smiling slowly, nodded her head in the direction of the demonstration. Claire knew something serious was wrong. She couldn't help herself so looked down to see her brothers being circled by a crowd of men holding weapons. They were moving closer to them by the second. Claire's eyes alternated from the grotesque Goth-roach to her brothers. She had to make a decision, and quickly.

'Damn,' she said to no one in particular. She quickly left the hideous creature, intent on saving her brothers.

They were already in trouble by the time Claire arrived. Jim was on his feet but Tony was curled up on the ground in the foetus position, unnervingly still. Claire dispensed with the minor evils as if they were nothing but irritating flies. As she suspected, these humans were both cowards and bullies. The man who'd started the attack screamed when a punch seemed to have come from nowhere. His mates were astounded when he fell over in agony clutching his groin. Two others followed suit and seeing their mates writhing around on the floor obviously in agony, the other nine thought it time to grab their friends and cut their losses.

'Wankers,' said one as he tried to help one of his fallen mates. 'You haven't heard the last of this.' His head bent back at the force of the invisible strike. The other men watched agog, as his nose appeared to spread and his eye swelled up and shut.

'Want some more?' said Jim, knowing Claire was their saviour even though she hadn't spoken.

The tables had turned as their assailants were now the victims, and were terrified by their invisible attacker. Jim was too worried about Tony to have some real fun with them as they scurried away. As he looked down at his brother, the adrenaline from the fight left his body in an instant.

'He's unconscious but he'll be okay. Call an ambulance.' Jim carried out his sister's instructions on autopilot.

By the time Tony woke up in hospital Claire was long gone. His head was bandaged and his face damaged and swollen, but Jim was relieved now he was awake. Losing his brother would be like losing a part of himself. He was terrified at the thought.

'How are you feeling?' Jim knew it was a stupid question but his emotions were all over the place, and he needed reassurance.

Tony heard the fear in his brother's voice although he'd tried to hide it.

'Every time I tried to check out, Claire's annoying voice told me I wasn't going anywhere,' he attempted a weak laugh to lighten the mood, but grimaced when he felt the pain in his ribs. 'I'm okay, bro.'

'They're keeping you in for a bit and Libby's on her way. She thinks we were mugged. I'll tell her they got my wallet but you had a good kicking because you wouldn't hand yours over.'

'Great, so I'll get a bollocking for being stupid as well as being in agony.' This time he managed not to laugh.

'But then she'll think you're a hero.' Jim went to tousle his brother's hair and pulled his hand back when he remembered the bandage. They smiled at each other, normal service resumed.

Libby arrived shortly after and they were surprised to see she was accompanied by their mother.

Tony reassured his tearful wife that he was going to be okay. They all agreed she'd leave Marion's to look after her husband when he left hospital.

'How is Val?' asked Tony and they reluctantly explained there hadn't been any improvement.

'Perhaps Fiona could take some time off work and give me a hand for a week?' said Marion.

'She's on a course, Mum and can't leave it at the moment.' Looking at his mother Jim thought she looked positively glowing with health compared to the last time he'd seen her when she'd been tired and run down.

'You're looking well.'

'The reunion in Yorkshire did your mother the world of good,' said Libby.

'What reunion?' the twins spoke together.

'Never mind that. Is Fiona's career that important that she can't take time off to be with her family when there's a crisis?'

Something's up thought Jim as his mother had avoided their question by changing the subject.

'Perhaps Carl can come and help with your mother?' said Jim and Libby tried not to smirk. Marion took the hint.

'Okay, point taken. You're right, Jim and he is Val's son after all. You may be surprised to hear that I've actually suggested that and he does call often. She doesn't want him to see her in her current condition though, so she refuses even to talk to him.'

'None of us can understand what's going on in Mum's head, it's really hard.'

Tony held his wife's hand. He felt guilty for causing her even more worry.

'It'll be fine, Libby. Really.' Unfortunately he didn't believe it would be fine. Neither did the others.

Marion and Jim left the room to give Tony and Libby some privacy.

'What's new with you then, Mum?'

'Nothing, Son. Same old, same old really.'

'Who's the new man?'

Jim saw the flicker of surprise on his mother's face before she managed to mask it. He knew he'd hit the nail on the head.

'Don't be ridiculous, there isn't a man. New or otherwise for that matter.'

'Mum, we're adults and have been for a long time. You don't need to hide it from us; it's pretty obvious you've got a new fella. Is he someone we know? Is that why you can't tell us? Or is it too early for you to know where the relationship is going...'

'All right all right. Stop with all the questions...'

'Well?'

She sighed in resignation. 'No he's not anyone you know and no, it's not too early. We both know where the relationship is going.'

Jim didn't need to ask any further questions. He could see how happy she looked when she talked about her new man. She also seemed relieved now it was out in the open.

'I'm pleased for you, Mum.'

She hugged him. 'Thanks, son. That means a lot to me. You can tell your brother and Libby but do it when I'm not there. I don't want you all to make a big deal of it.'

It was a big deal but Jim knew his mother didn't like a fuss. After what had happened with their father, and Val's experience with the villain, his mother was wary and distrustful of most men. If she'd fallen for someone he was reasonably confident he must be a good bloke, or patient and trustworthy at the very least. Still, Jim would feel happier once they'd met him.

'Who is he and when will we...'

'One step at a time, son.'

He didn't want to push too hard so resisted the urge to ask anything further.

*****

Val couldn't believe they'd left her on her own. She'd protested but Marion had been firm, telling her she still had the use of her arms and legs, and could look after herself for a few hours. Val knew that Tony had been hurt, but he had his brother to look after him and Marion could have stayed with her at the very least. She wasn't in the right frame of mind to wonder how she would have felt if Carl had been attacked. Instead she wallowed in self-pity, eventually crying herself to sleep.

Peace evaded her and the dream felt so real.

Chapter 17

Grant knew that if he didn't turn his life around soon it would be too late. He had been shocked the previous morning when he woke up with the usual hangover, but with a voice in his head that felt as real as his own. He thought he was going nuts so had considered his choices; wallow in self-pity, alcohol and go mad, or get a grip. He chose the latter. This time he would go it alone and not trust anyone. Grant felt better having made his decision. The next few days were spent shopping for supplies and avoiding alcohol. Using an undercover identity and false driving licence to hire a car, he loaded his surveillance gear and camping kit. He wasn't the outdoorsy type so had bought a lightweight tent that was easy to erect, as well as the warmest sleeping bag available. He planned to sleep in the car on the journey up to Scotland, using the facilities in the Services to eat and keep himself clean. He envisaged he would only need to sleep out in the wilds during one night when he couldn't take the car too near to the facility. He felt much better about himself now he was taking positive action. Having been discredited he knew that no respectable paper in the UK would touch him with a barge pole. He also knew they loved a good story over the pond so that's where he would try to sell his – he was convinced there was an interesting tale to be told about the facility that wasn't what it pretended to be.

Grant managed to avoid all human company on his journey and two days later he used his state of the art camera to take close up photographs. His presence was undiscovered so he clicked away to his heart's content as he watched the few vehicles coming and going. The trouble was that the photographs showed the outside of a building, but not what went on inside. Grant's intention was to visit the secure psychiatric facility down south again, and compare photographs. He hoped his tagline: *What Is This Place?* Would pique enough interest for someone to buy the article.

Remembering what had happened during his last visit, Grant didn't hang about longer than necessary and made his way home as soon as he'd finished. During his recce of the other secure facility, he noted an increase in traffic and that security patrols appeared to be more regular. Grant took his photographs quickly to avoid discovery. Now totally driven he dumped his kit in his bland bedsit. It was dark by the time he'd drafted the article before retiring to catch up on his sleep. The following morning he logged onto the Internet first thing to check out various publications. Mission complete, Grant was ready to approach his contacts in the USA.

He had good reason to be paranoid so used a number of different URLs to send and receive his messages from a newly created email account. Despite a number of rejections over the next few days he was determined not to give up. His persistence paid off. It had taken three days but eventually a medium-sized publication agreed to run with his story. The pay barely covered his expenses but Grant wanted to restore his reputation and money hadn't been the object of the exercise. When the story broke a small town decided to run it on their news channel. An ex-MI5 whistle-blower was asked his opinion and his views gave Grant's story the credibility he'd craved.

*****

Violet, Professor Robert, Ryan, Janine and Mr Smart were waiting in the Director's outer office while he was on the phone. The PA's phone buzzed then she asked them all to go in.

'That was the Home Secretary's office. He's just returned from the select Cobra meeting.' The others knew that *select* was code for the elite number of Cobra members who held the highest security clearance. 'They're moving a few of the more dangerous offenders up here to convince the public that we really are a secure facility for the criminally insane.' His face remained neutral as he spoke but Violet knew his true feelings on the matter.

When the story had hit the news the previous day the Director had expected an over-reaction, even though he'd advised the Home Secretary against any knee-jerk response.

'This is it, Violet. You know that, don't you?'

Much as she'd hated to admit it, she agreed with her husband. These things had a habit of taking their own course. She felt that whatever action they took to stop the true identity of the school from being discovered would ultimately fail. The momentum would build now the article had been published and the seeds planted in the public's imagination. That's why they had tried so hard to discredit the journalist. Violet brought herself back to the present as her husband addressed the meeting.

'Do they really think they can still hoodwink everyone now the story's out?'

'I agree entirely, Robert,' the Director opened his hands. 'Ours is not to reason why...'

Mr Smart raised his concerns regarding his manpower.

'A unit's being sent to us specifically for this purpose, Smarty,' he swallowed before continuing. 'Unfortunately, you need to brief them and then hand over control...'

'No way, Director. I don't...'

'I'm sorry but that's the way it is. Officially your role will be in an advisory capacity only, but we'll discuss this further outside of this meeting.'

Mr Smart calmed down knowing that his official role and what the Director wanted him to do were two different matters entirely.

The Director gave them further details telling them the serial killer known as *Mad Martin* would arrive within the week. There was silence as the others contemplated the fact they'd be in the same building as the country's most violent and sadistic killer. Some said he was mad, others pure evil and many of the details regarding the way he'd butchered thirteen women had been withheld from publication, having been considered too horrific for the public to stomach.

'An advance party of the security unit will oversee the preparations of his accommodation. When everything is to their satisfaction they'll bring him here under heavy escort and he'll be accommodated in *A Wing*. The work from that wing will be moved to the spare sections in *B Wing*.'

The meeting finished, each attendee, except Ryan, having been given their specific tasks in preparation for the arrival of the new inmate. Ryan was to team up with Jim until Tony returned to active duty.

*****

'I'm coming to get you, Val. We will be together.'

'Leave me alone, you're a pervert, a paedophile and a total waste of space.'

He laughed and it wasn't the laugh she'd remembered when he was alive, but a cruel, harsh sound that promised future pain.

'We are meant for each other, Val. There's no point fighting it…'

She woke up in a sweat, her heart beating so hard it felt as if it would break out of her body. Val looked around half expecting to see Gary standing in front of her, still laughing. The curtains fanned out and blew as if in a gale, but the air was still as silence, until

175

Val screamed. If anyone heard her on the busy outer-city street, they didn't show it as they hurried about their business. As Marion unlocked the door she thought her friend must be under attack. She hurried to the kitchen arming herself with a sharp knife before rushing up the stairs as quickly but stealthily as she could. Marion was surprised to see Val was alone in the room. She calmed herself and looked at her friend as she rushed to her side. Her unwashed hair was sticking out in all directions - her eyes obviously seeing something that Marion couldn't. Marion put the knife down on the dressing table and held her friend until she stopped shaking. She thought fleetingly that Val looked like an extra from an old horror movie. It was impossible for her to understand Val's incoherent babbling so she held her and made soothing noises until her panicking subsided.

*****

Claire needed to regain her strength. She judged she still had it in her to capture some of the weaker evils, but knew she'd be in trouble if she encountered any stronger or cleverer. As she returned to Cherussola Claire wondered eagerly whether Raphael would be awake. Disappointed there was no change, she rushed to Gabriella's then Amanda's quarters to discover them both empty. Unable to find anyone to explain, Claire requested an audience with the Committee. She was politely refused.

'What O, old girl.'

Claire jumped at hearing the now familiar voice, then smiled. Hopefully Zach knew what was going on.

'All's well here and our new recruits are doing marvellously.'

'Glad to hear it, Zach, but why isn't Raphael awake? And what about Gabriella and Amanda, where are they...'

'I know, I know. The good and the great have asked me to explain. Come and have a seat.' This last was spoken tenderly and Claire shivered with foreboding. Although totally drained there was no way she could rest without hearing what Zach had to say.

'Please, Zach. What is it?'

'You know it was touch and go with my recovery?'

She nodded, impatient to hear more. 'Well, if I hadn't have come round I would have been sent to heaven for eternity.'

'In that comatose rest state?'

'I wouldn't call it that exactly, but yes, that's the gist of it.'

'So are you saying that if Raphael doesn't wake up that's it? Whoosh. He'll be sent to heaven and I'll never see him again?'

Zach heard the panic in her voice so enveloped her in a much-needed embrace. It didn't make her feel any better but at least quelled the panic as she thought of Raphael lying there having no idea of who or where he was. Zach didn't tell her about the memories of torture he'd had whilst he was recovering, or that some of the events had played over and over again as if they were real. Claire hadn't said anything about her own memories of Hell so he hoped that was just his own experience and Raphael wasn't going through the same. In any case, he had no intention of making her feel any worse. She seemed to have calmed down so he continued.

'At least he's safe, my dear. You can join him in your quarters shortly. I'm certain that if anyone can help bring him back, Claire, it's you.' He'd managed to avoid answering her question, for now anyway.

'What of Gabriella and Amanda?' she knew she should ask about them but only half listened as Zach explained, still too upset to stop thinking about Raphael.

'Unfortunately, Claire, they shouldn't have come looking for you and left all this,' he indicated the area with a swing of his arm, 'vulnerable to attack. You know what's happened since and the Committee have demoted them.' It would be adding insult to injury to tell her Raphael would also be demoted if he awoke, so he decided against it.

'Where are they?'

'It seems the speed of our recovery is related to how many evils are loose in the atmosphere. Amanda is gathering the evils like there's no tomorrow and dumping them in the cave. Gabriella is of course conducting the whole operation.'

'My operation?'

So she still had enough gumption to care about the operation, despite the news of Raphael. 'Now, now, Claire. Being possessive isn't a very angel-like characteristic is it?'

Suitably chastised she waited for him to continue.

'We all received instructions from the Committee while you were working hard down there. You are to carry on with what you're doing, but when it comes to picking off the stronger evils, we have to plan it carefully and assist each other. That's when the lovely Gabriella will come into play. She's whooshing around providing the back up and strength as required.'

His earlier words sunk in and Claire knew she had to get back to work to catch more evils. She shook her head trying to fight her fatigue. Zach could see what she was attempting.

'Steady on, Claire. I can't let you leave until you're fully refreshed. You go and rest now then when

178

you come back, you can go after the deformed creature you left in order to save your brothers.'

'Who put you in charge?' but as she said it she knew he was right so disappeared shortly after. The sooner she rested the sooner she'd be able to resume the fight, which had become even more crucial to her own happiness and Raphael's survival.

*****

The Home Secretary's Office had been informed of the transportation plans for Mad Martin. The Private Secretary had written a memo to his boss notifying him that a military transporter would take the convict to Inverness by air, and the onward journey to the facility would be under armed escort. The busy Home Secretary assumed the escort from Inverness would also involve military personnel. It was a wise decision as there had been a few recent and embarrassing mishaps with Lyton Security, the newly contracted security company. Satisfied with the arrangements he signed off the memo as he went about his other business.

During the flight Mad Martin knew there was no means of escape but that didn't stop him from sussing out his surroundings just in case an opportunity arose. As usual, whenever he travelled he was shackled. This time they'd chained him to his seat as if he were a rabid animal who they feared might escape. One thing about these military types was they took their duties seriously so there was no way he could move out of his seat without their assistance. He'd been forced to use the toilet at the airport and when he'd asked to go on the plane one of his military guards had been unsympathetic, telling him to tie a knot in it. The other thing about these guys was that he couldn't intimidate them like he could some of the civilians. Out of sheer boredom he'd tried giving them all the evil eye but none had shown the usual expected fear. The one that

179

spoke in a scouse accent had even smiled at him. Martin was pissed off he didn't even have the upper hand with visual intimidation, which was his only possible means of control. He caught the eye of one of the civilian guards and the other man soon looked away making him feel slightly better. He'd hoped there would be at least one woman on the journey but there wasn't and he was unsure if that was by design or coincidence. He closed his eyes letting his mind wander to better days when there had been women, and they were the ones wearing the shackles. He longed to feel that sense of absolute power again. Smiling to himself he remembered their looks of sheer terror as he carried out his work. The only similarity his thirteen victims had in common was the way they looked at him before he started chopping. Their eyes were always the last to go and the fear had long since left by the time he removed them from their sockets. He was mentally dissecting victim number three when he was rudely prodded, jolting him back to his current unsatisfactory reality. They had a change of mind, allowing him to use the toilet before leaving the plane. Sitting down to piss did nothing to improve his mood. It was humiliating, especially being stared at while doing so.

A black van with tinted windows was brought to the edge of the runway. Mad Martin was manhandled from the aircraft into the back of the van where they secured him before speeding off. The two civilian guards who had been on the plane were in the back with him.

As the van left the airport other road users were totally unaware of its passenger who sat in the back, chained like an animal. Only a small number of people knew about the journey, together with a number of unearthly, uninvited passengers now in and around the vehicle. Mad Martin sensed the dark presence. The other occupants felt tense and uncomfortable, assuming it was due to the presence of the evil and sadistic serial killer.

Big Ed was pleased with his choice of host this time. He could feel the man's body was strong and not poisoned by drugs or alcohol. The guy obviously worked out but hadn't been allowed to become too bulky. That would be a potential problem for his jailers. He wasn't worried about the man's mind because he would eventually control it. Not yet powerful enough to stay in the host body all the time, Big Ed knew he'd need to pace himself until he was. Only then could he carry out his plan. In the meantime he would get this maniac to do his bidding. When he wasn't with him he would visit Val as often as he could, to remind her of what her future held. But first there was the little matter of escape. He summoned his dark helpers and issued instructions.

Mad Martin's beady black eyes flicked from side to side but all he could see were the guards and the insides of his mobile prison. His eyes came to rest on one of his guards. He smiled at the man as he imagined cutting him open and pulling out his insides while he was still alive.

The evil maniac was making the big guard feel uncomfortable so he looked away and checked his weapon. The guard had heard a number of do-gooders say nobody was all bad. Well none of these had looked directly into the eyes of Mad Martin. He kept telling himself there was no way the evil beast could escape, but whatever it was he'd felt since getting in the van had multiplied as the journey progressed. He was nervous as hell. He checked his weapon again, patting it to make himself feel better.

Mad Martin noticed the guard patting his weapon continuously and delighted in the fact he could still frighten them, despite being chained up like Houdini prior to performing one of his stunts.

They came off the motorway onto an A road. One of the guards radioed the driver requesting a comfort break.

The driver looked at his hands as they left the steering wheel then at his colleague in the passenger seat in utter surprise.

'What the hell are you doing?' shouted the colleague as he leaned over to grab the steering wheel, but it was too late. Those in the back of the van felt it lose control and their world went into slow motion.

The chains initially held Mad Martin in place for the first roll of the vehicle but the guards weren't so fortunate. One had removed his seatbelt and stood up to stretch right at the time the vehicle lost control. He was now unconscious having been flung about the van like pyjamas in a washing machine. The other was still in his seat with a piece of broken glass sticking out of the side of his head.

As the vehicle came to a rest one of Mad Martin's arm chains had come loose but the other was still firmly in place. The voice in his head was urging him on and he knew he had limited time to escape. He could just about reach the first guard. With super human effort he dragged the unconscious man by the belt on his waist so he could reach all of his pockets. There were only two keys on the key ring he found; they unlocked his leg chains, but not his arms. Legs now unchained he could easily reach the other guard but it took a few minutes for him to manoeuvre his feet into a position where he could use them to unlock the seat belt. This completed he pushed the body forward so he could wrap the lower part of his legs around the guard. It took a herculean effort for him to drag the body near enough to reach the keys. Once he did he unlocked his arms and jumped out of the open back door. Much as he wanted to inflict serious pain on his captors, he knew he had limited time in which to make his escape. They were in the middle of nowhere and he jumped back into the van to get the weapon that the guard had been patting. He fired a round into each head, went to the front of the van and did the same with the unconscious driver and passenger. Trying to think calmly he wasted time looking for the key that would unlock the bulky electronic tagging device secured around his right ankle. He struggled to remove it to no avail then using the metal housing that was attached to one of his chains, he battered it until the light went out. It would slow him down but he knew he didn't have any more time to waste; he'd heard them check in every fifteen minutes and knew at least six had passed since the crash.

Mad Martin made his way cross-country. By the time the police helicopters and search teams had been mustered he had already broken into his first car. He'd decided to head north until the voice in his head told him otherwise. *We're going back to London* it said and he was shocked the voice was really there, not merely a figment of his imagination. When he'd refused to listen first of all, the steering wheel turned heading the car toward the grass verge. Martin knew he'd moved the wheel but he also knew he hadn't been able to help himself. He changed direction and banged on the wheel in frustration, a free man now but still not in control of his own destiny. He was frightened. Whoever was in his head was a meaner bastard than he was.

Chapter 18

Feeling totally rested and refreshed Claire was ready for action. There was still no movement from Raphael so she was determined to catch as many evils as possible hoping it would help to speed up his recovery. He would recover, she knew that and wouldn't allow herself to think any differently; the consequences were too dire. She had an unusual feeling in her back but tried not to dwell on it, as she needed to focus on finishing what she'd started with Goth-roach. Her next priority was to visit her brothers to check on Tony's progress. She felt herself travelling faster than before and soon encountered some disorganised evils. The first wave didn't cause her much bother but then she ran into a gang who were following the teenager Harry. Claire initially proceeded with caution. She knew Harry was weak and cowardly, but also knew his son could put in an appearance at any time. The way things were these days meant she could be safe one moment and in dire danger the next. When not in Cherussola Claire sometimes felt like a small animal always on the look out in case of predators. Feeling nostalgic she remembered her early death days with fondness recalling that Gabriella always had her back, and she hadn't experienced the fear and wariness that were now her constant companions. Sometimes ignorance was bliss. While reminiscing Claire made a schoolgirl error. Harry's son was nowhere to be seen. Without him she expected Harry and his gang to be a bunch of weak losers. Claire's earlier caution disappeared. Her confidence soared and she convinced herself she would overcome the enemy despite being alone. She was in for an unpleasant surprise. Harry was clearly the leader and his strategy was both intelligent and decisive. Claire had to concentrate all her efforts as the physical blows rained down on her. Despite the pain she rallied, regretting her misplaced confidence at the same time. It was touch and go. What surprised her more than the pain was when she heard a familiar whoosh that had been absent for too long. There was no intervention so Claire focused, knowing her mentor was watching. Always better with an audience she upped her game. Claire eventually regained the advantage feeling more powerful than ever. There was no smugness when she overcame the evils; it had been too close to call. Harry disappeared shouting his usual tirade of abuse and the words remained a lot longer than he did. The fight over, Claire centred herself.

'Gabriella, welcome back.'

When she turned she tried unsuccessfully to hide her shock at Gabriella's appearance. Her face was as beautiful as ever but she looked haunted. Her arms had lumps gouged out of them and what looked like teeth marks. Claire gasped but Gabriella smiled.

'You may not think so, Claire, but you were one of the lucky ones.' Seeing that she was still upset she added softly. 'The physical marks will fade over time but not until the equilibrium is restored. You've done a great job so far.'

'Oh, Gabriella.' Overcome by her emotions she flung herself at her mentor, for once totally speechless.

They hugged and Gabriella was as happy to see her young apprentice but didn't feel the need to tell her. She loosened Claire's hold putting a little space between them.

'I'm so proud of what you've achieved while we've been otherwise engaged,' her eyes twinkled. 'But I'm back now so you don't have to bear that responsibility any longer.

'But…'

'Congratulations, by the way.' Gabriella nodded towards Claire's back.

When Claire looked over her own shoulder she felt like jumping for joy. She turned back to Gabriella and the senior angel gave an encouraging nod.

So that explained the feeling she'd had earlier she thought as she tried out the newly formed wings, flapping each in turn. It was all too much to take in at once as she realised she was now a fully-fledged junior angel. She wondered what would change and what else would be expected of her. Would she be allowed to carry on as before? If so, why hadn't anyone told her that this was going to happen?

Gabriella knew Claire had many questions.

'Zach and I had a word with the Committee before I left. You've impressed them, Claire.'

Gabriella didn't add that the Committee had given her a severe reprimand for what they called her foolhardy rescue mission. She was lucky the world was in turmoil and they'd decided to go easy on her for now, due to extenuating circumstances. She snapped back to the present.

'Everything will become clear in due course, Claire. But now we have work to do.'

'I can handle it, Gabriella. I've managed for long enough thus far.' She wiggled her new wings unnecessarily, unable to resist the urge.

Gabriella could just about remember the brilliant feeling of being bestowed with wings. Not only the extra physical power they provided but the instant respect from both good and evil spirits, albeit for different reasons. But the most overriding and powerful feeling had been the sense of elation when realising the Committee had put their trust in her for eternity. Certain that Claire wasn't aware she was one of only the chosen two per cent, Gabriella decided that now wasn't the time or place.

'Why fight alone when you don't need to?'

'But...'

'Is this about your ego or about saving the world, Claire?'

She'd hit the nail on the head and Claire explained why she had unfinished business with Goth-roach.

'She should be easy to find at least.' Gabriella's eyes twinkled and her lips twitched. She couldn't help laughing despite the seriousness of their situation. Claire realised how much she'd missed hearing the hearty laugh that didn't match its owner. She joined in and the noise reverberated through the atmosphere as the two angels sped towards their next big fight.

*****

The Director was furious when the new Private Secretary told him about Mad Martin's escape. He was in his office, relaying the gist of the conversation to Violet. '*It will take the heat off the school* he said. As if that would make me feel better for God's sake!' he banged his fist on the desk and Violet tried to remain calm while he got it out of his system.

'One of the most dangerous, no, *the* most dangerous serial killer in this country is on the loose, and I'm supposed to feel relieved that the heat's off the school. What sort of people does he think we are for fuck's sake?' he shook his head. 'Oh, and it gets even better. There was some sort of communication mix up and they used Lyton Security - you know the ones that couldn't organise a...'

'You're kidding me?'

'I wish I was, Violet.' His tirade over he was now back to his usual, rational self. 'That's why it was a new PS that called. The last one, who's related to the head of Lyton Security by the way, has been suspended pending investigation. You couldn't make up this shit, could you?'

187

Violet rolled her eyes in agreement. 'Do they have any idea where he might be?'

'The search parties were deployed pretty quickly but he'd already disappeared. I'm sure he'll leave a trail.'

They both knew it wouldn't be long before some unfortunate souls would have their lives cut short by the evil serial killer. 'The Minister wants us to assist until the police operation is in full swing, then we'll stand down.' Violet gave him a *yeah-right* look. 'Get Fiona to round up as many agents as she can. It'll be quicker if we travel to them.' Back in business mode, the Director put arrangements in hand for the meeting to take place in Birmingham early the following morning.

*****

Mad Martin didn't know the name of the town he was in, nor did he care. He needed food and money. It was bloody cold so he'd need to act soon. The voice in his head told him their best bet was to break into a house and the cold weather was on their side. He parked the car out of sight and made his way to a residential area. Nobody was about as he looked through a window into a detached bungalow at the end of a quiet street. A middle-aged woman was putting on her coat and talking to an old lady who was sitting in a chair trying to watch the TV as the other woman talked. The middle-aged woman said her goodbyes and kissed the older woman. Mad Martin disappeared around the side of the house before the front door opened, watching as the visitor got into her car and drove away. Returning to the window he continued watching as the woman drifted alternatively from wakefulness to sleep. As he licked his lips planning the fun he'd have with her, the voice in his head told him he'd do no such thing. When he tried to argue, his hand gave his face a severe slap. The slap shocked him and he gasped. He quickly shrank back from the window as the old woman opened her eyes for a second. Sensing there was worse to come if he disobeyed the voice, he hid for ten minutes then risked another look. She seemed to be sleeping peacefully and he was told that now was the time. He moved quietly to the back of the house and tried the kitchen door. It was locked of course so he moved to the window. The bungalow was in need of renovation so it took little effort to break the rusty lock. He was as quiet as he could be but there was still a noise. Mad Martin waited to see if the woman would call or make an appearance. Even with the kitchen door closed he could hear the television so perhaps she hadn't looked earlier, and was deaf or hard of hearing. He opened the door slowly, smiling to himself as he heard her gentle snores. She knew very little about her death a few seconds later, as the chain was tightened around her neck and she was taken before her time.

The voice told him they'd be safe for a while but Mad Martin knew this anyway. He was told to eat and rest and didn't want to incur its wrath so obeyed the instructions. It was still dark when he woke. Opening his eyes he awaited his next orders. It took him a few seconds to realise the voice wasn't there. He went to the kitchen to make a coffee, trying to ignore the temptation of Mrs McDonald's body as he waited for the voice to return. Unable to resist any longer he sneaked a peep through the kitchen door and started fantasising about what he could do to the old woman, all the time expecting a verbal or physical reprimand. When none was forthcoming the urge was too much for Mad Martin. Impatiently he emptied the kitchen drawers licking his lips as he grabbed three sharp knives and approached her, feeling as if all his birthdays and Christmases had come at once.

*****

Besides the obvious outward appearance, Claire was beginning to realise that having wings was a distinct advantage. Now an integral part of her they were sensitive, like a sort of spiritual antennae, and she was learning to pick up signals depending on how they felt. Gabriella's reaction from her own wings had long been second nature, but she coached Claire in the hope she would quickly become expert. Every time Gabriella sensed evil in the atmosphere she waited until Claire could identify it and Claire was learning quickly. They encountered swarms of evils on their way to find Goth-roach. When they eventually sighted her, she was still in her spirit form. They had no misconceptions it would be an easy fight so watched from a distance first of all, trying to discover how much support she actually had. Claire explained what had happened during the first fight including why she'd had to leave. Gabriella was in no position to reprimand her for helping her brothers but Claire was still pleasantly surprised that she hadn't. She noticed a number of changes in their relationship, the main being that Gabriella was treating her more as an equal. Claire put this down to her wings and gave them a little wiggle. Gabriella sighed inwardly and outwardly shook her head.

'Here goes.'

Some of the more powerful evils could sense changes in the atmosphere and Claire's wing wiggle had given their presence away. They watched as the evil spirit turned into her physical form. Gabriella baulked as she looked at the hideous creature.

'Actually, Claire, her physical countenance perfectly matches her evil personality. You've inadvertently done a good job on her and caused her lots of aggravation by the looks of it.'

They watched as some of the braver or more stupid subordinates laughed at her form and tormented her. She soon became apoplectic and their ribaldry turned to fear as they stopped laughing when she directed her fury at them.

'Incoming,' shouted Gabriella. 'Dodge to the right.'

Claire obeyed instinctively. The junior evil missed her by a hair's breadth as it whizzed passed screaming and wailing.

'Hell hath no fury like a woman...err, turned into an insect,' she said as she followed Gabriella toward the evils, dodging those who had insulted the Goth-roach as they went.

By the time her fury was spent the evils that remained with Goth-roach did so out of fear rather than any sense of loyalty. Claire started gathering them to deliver to the cave along with their mistress, and put a force field around those she captured. Gabriella spotted a few trying to escape and added her strength to the force field. None of the others were a match for her power as she pulled them toward her. Despite their screaming and punching there was nothing they could do. All the while they dealt with the minors, they were dodging the objects being thrown by their mistress and trying to ignore the constant stream of obscenities. Goth-roach found herself alone in the fight she knew she couldn't win without support. It was not in her nature to surrender so she called for assistance. The new wave that appeared were dispensed with matter of factly, to be harnessed in the force field along with the others. They repeated the process until Goth-roach called and nobody came. Claire was exhausted and looked to Gabriella. The senior angel seemed to ooze both peace and energy and Claire took her lead from her, unaware that Gabriella was as tired as she was. Goth-roach looked around deciding it was time to disappear. She didn't get far before the angels drew her toward them. As much as she screamed and kicked they continued to draw her in, eventually delivering her to the holding area with the others. Frustrated and furious she intended to inflict as much pain and suffering on her own kind as she could. The fighting over Gabriella held out her hand to Claire and closed with their captives, forming a circle around them. They closed their eyes visualising the cockroach form. Goth-roach was the first to change. All screaming stopped as her head soon matched the form of its body. The remainder followed quickly, those not already showing in their human form changed to that first, then to cockroaches from the toes up. The heads were always the last to change and each watched their own transformation in horror, knowing their eternity would be spent in this hideous form.

*****

Mad Martin looked up from the mess he'd made of Mrs McDonald with no more compassion than a lion viewing its latest kill. He was tired from the cutting and chopping, but a satisfied tired. It had been too long since the last time and he wiped his bloody hands on his prison trousers before unbuttoning them to deal with his arousal.

'What the fuck's going on you sick bastard.' The voice in his head screamed. This time his hand balled into a fist and punched his face, following it up with a few slaps about his head. As much as Big Ed wanted to punish his depraved host, he knew that he needed his body to be in a reasonably fit state to carry out his work.

'Get yourself cleaned up. Now!'

Mad Martin's high disappeared and terrified, he rushed to obey his captor's orders in fear of physical reprisals if he disobeyed. He ran upstairs to the small bathroom and showered using the old-fashioned shower attachment over the bath. Smelling of lavender soap and sin he wrapped the towel around his waist while he emptied Mrs McDonald's wardrobe. There was nothing suitable and the voice was becoming more and more impatient. Noticing a suitcase on top of the wardrobe Mad Martin struck lucky. He found some men's clothing inside. Putting on the trousers he felt something in the pocket and his hand pulled out a wad of ten-pound notes. He allowed himself a small smile before the voice told him to get on with it. The trousers were baggy but a belt did the job and he wasn't bothered the old grey sweatshirt didn't match the brown trousers. Clean and ready to leave Mad Martin rushed down the stairs just as a shadow appeared in the glass of the front door, followed by a voice.

'Coooeee, are you there, Flo?'

He rubbed his hands together looking skyward, thanking his maker for sending him another victim.

'It's not going to happen,' this time the voice was a sinister whisper and it directed Mad Martin to the brass soldier ornament on the mantelpiece in the lounge. He picked it up while creeping to the front door as instructed. The woman was banging on the door now, telling Flo that if she didn't open up she would get someone to help break it down. Mad Martin took a deep breath – the voice had told him he had to be quick and he'd be severely punished if this went wrong.

He pulled open the door. The woman's mouth was half-open about to speak until she realised it wasn't Flo. A quick glance showed there was nobody else on the street so he grabbed her with one hand, while bringing the force of the brass soldier down on her head with the other. The woman was unconscious before she had the chance to scream and she slumped to the floor. He kicked the door closed with his foot and dragged the visitor into the lounge, dumping her unceremoniously on the floor. Following the instructions of the voice he left by the back door and head down, quickly made his was to his car to resume the journey south.

*****

News of Mad Martin's escape was all over the media together with the news that a minister's aide had been sacked due to his association with Lyton Security. The Director and Violet had been wrong about the demise of the school – the escape had taken the heat off the facility as the general public were understandably distressed such a dangerous killer was on the loose. He'd assigned his agents at the meeting in Birmingham, and Ryan and Jim were working together. Tony was making a good recovery but was still on sick leave due to his injury. The Director's PA buzzed to inform him that Ryan was now on the secure phone.

'We've found a body and a car that was stolen not far from where he escaped.'

At long last a breakthrough, thought the Director but nothing to smile about. 'Okay, give me the details.'

Ryan explained they were in the countryside about ten miles outside the border town of Ailkirk, where the police were already carrying out a house-to-house search due to a woman's disappearance. 'I know it's a stretch but we wondered if he might have something to do with her disappearance, but it's a man's body,' he quickly added. 'No signs of a struggle so whoever stole the car obviously didn't want anyone to find it, due to its location.' Ryan was careful not to assume that Mad Martin had stolen the car; police forensics would determine that.

'Right, I'll put the police onto your discovery and get the dead man identified. All we know from this is that he's made his way southwards but we guessed he'd do that anyway. We're not much further forward so I may have to rethink our strategy. I'll be in touch.' It went without saying that Ryan would contact the Director if there were any further developments so they hung up. It wasn't much later that the Director received the call telling him about the gruesome

194

discovery of Mrs McDonald and her unfortunate friend. He was also informed that the police were now in full control of the operation.

'The police constable who found her will need counselling I'm told,' the Director said to Violet, 'but it's no longer our business.' Violet raised her eyebrows.

'I know. We need to see what else we can do to stop this evil maniac, unofficially of course.'

She agreed. As they discussed their options, they both knew there was only one possible way forward.

*****

Claire had mixed feelings as they neared the cave. It meant another mission was over and she'd soon return to Cherussola. Every time she returned she'd been full of hope that Raphael had come back to her, only to be disappointed at the reality of the situation. They dropped off the cockroaches with the bat guardians.

'You look done in,' said Ron. Despite everything she'd been through, Claire still found it difficult communicating with him in his bat guise.

'Cat got your tongue?'

She shook herself out of it. 'No. I'm just tired as you say. Err, how are you finding it?'

'Well, I can't say that it's a particularly enjoyable duty and you know how it stinks in here. But we're doing our bit,' he nodded towards Sandy. 'We know it won't be for ever.'

'Sooner than you think, Ron, actually.'

'How so, Gabriella?' it was Claire who asked the question.

'I need you back to help me process...some new spirits.'

'Oh, we expected to be here for longer. I thought you had plenty of help now?'

'Just you, Ron, Sandy's staying put for now.'

195

Sandy looked disappointed but said nothing. Claire could see Ron was trying to process the information and so was she.

'What's going...'

'Not now, Claire. We need to get some rest and you know we're more vulnerable if we're too tired. The change will exhaust Ron too so let's get a move on.'

It was true. In their current condition they'd be hard pushed to fight off a full-scale attack if they were jumped on their way back. Even so, Claire knew Gabriella had kept something back. She fully intended to find out more as soon as she was rested. Indeed, this might be the time Raphael awoke she thought hopefully, as she prepared to leave.

Gabriella disappeared as soon as they returned, depriving Claire of any opportunity to ask questions. Ron was fighting to keep his eyes open so it was no good asking his thoughts about the sudden recall. They said their goodbyes and when she returned to their quarters the room had changed. One wall was rich teal, her favourite colour, and there was a beautiful autumn picture hanging on another pale green wall. All was calm and Claire could hear the sound of the ocean in the distance. Gabriella had told her that angels were able to choose their scenery in Cherussola. Claire realised she must have done this without any conscious effort. She would have been overjoyed with her new surroundings had all been well. But Raphael was lying on the bed as still as the last time she'd seen him. Claire ran her hands over his scars then stroked his chest. No reaction. She kissed his cheek first then his lips, moving down his body kissing and caressing as she went. Nothing. She sighed and curled up next to him, staring at him while willing him to open his eyes with all her being. Eventually her exhaustion got the better of her so she let it take her where there was no pain or worry.

Claire didn't know how much later it was when she felt the touch. She thought she was dreaming a dream that couldn't come true while Raphael was lost to her. It had been so long since they'd made love and she let the dream take her to paradise as she felt his firm hands explore her body tentatively at first, before becoming more confident. The kisses started on her neck then worked their way downwards. She woke when she felt herself being flipped over onto her stomach. Claire had no idea what he was doing to her wings, only that she didn't want it to stop. When he did her senses were so heightened that his every touch sent delicious shock waves through her entire being. He nuzzled the small gap in between her wings, before moving his tongue down the length of her. She opened up to him and he took her from behind, slow and masterful at first, then with an urgency that made her cry out in ecstasy. Her cry was for the magic of the moment and the fact that her beautiful angel had at long last returned. There was no need for words as they enjoyed each other over and over, revelling in the love and passion that had been absent for too long. Eventually spent, they slept, holding each other tightly so nothing could come between them.

Claire was full of optimism when she awoke, believing anything was possible now that Raphael was with her. Her kisses woke him.

'I love you so much,' she ran a hand over the scars that already seemed to be fading. 'But what have they done to you?' Although his physical injuries weren't as bad as his sister's, she knew he must have suffered immeasurably to have been so close to never waking. Claire wondered if the worse had happened to him after she'd been rescued.

'I'm going to be all right, Claire, these will heal.' He looked at the marks on his arms and legs that were worse on his right side.

She assumed a violent attack had taken him by surprise and wanted to know more.

'How did...' she stopped. His expression was full of pain and she held him tightly. It took a supreme effort for her not to push further. Naturally curious and madly in love, she had a compelling desire to discover everything that had happened to Raphael. It was too soon and Claire knew it wouldn't be easy for him to tell or for her to hear. Hoping to speed the healing process she kissed each scar again, and, for now, acquiesced to his wishes.

'I'm back and we're together and you'll never know how much that means to me.'

'I have an inkling.' her eyes twinkled with the memory of their lovemaking. Then he noticed a change in her expression.

'What is it?'

'There have been many changes since you've been away. I'm not sure how to tell you this…'

'Spill, Claire. Nothing can be worse than what we've already been through except for my light to be permanently distinguished. Thankfully that didn't happen.'

'Right then,' she closed her eyes for a second, wondering what would be the best way to tell him. Raphael waited patiently, as she looked at him she decided on the direct approach. 'I think you're going to be demoted and you'll probably have to spend time in the cave.'

'As a bat?'

'Yes, a bat.' He didn't look that bothered so Claire wondered if all his faculties had actually returned.

'What of my mother and Gabriella?'

Claire explained everything, including her feeling that something about Ron's early return didn't ring true.

'Clever girl,' he kissed the top of her head. 'But not quite clever enough.'

'Just tell me, now.'

He laughed as she waggled her beautiful wings in frustration. 'You know that patience is a virtue, my love.'

'Fine, Raphael. I'll find out my own way.'

Her attempt at calm serenity didn't fool him and he laughed as he pulled her into a hug. She couldn't be annoyed with him for long and she melted under his touch.'

'I've missed you so much.'

'You'll never know how glad I am to be back with you, Claire. Now, about Ron.'

She listened as he explained that someone's time was up. 'You know how scary death is so it's always better for new spirits to be met by someone they know. It sounds as if things are getting back to normal if Gabriella has arranged for him to meet someone.'

'But she must have a reason for not telling him who.'

Raphael waited for the penny to drop and Claire was astounded when it did. 'Val? You mean it's Val's time? But she isn't that old. What's going to happen? Ron will be devastated...'

He let her witter on until she ran out of questions.

'Ours is not to reason why, etcetera. Shall we go and see if we can find Gabriella?'

There was a double whoosh as they left. Claire determined that Gabriella would shed light on the mystery as soon as she woke up.

*****

The owner of voice hadn't had it all his own way. During the first days of his possession Mad Martin had struggled, trying his best to make it disappear. He now accepted that it would come and go of its own accord so had no choice but to live with it. He had tried to defy it on more than one occasion and his face and body paid the price for his disobedience. Still, he was by no means a pushover and on waking each day knew instantly whether the voice was with him. Unable to stifle his sadistic urges Mad Martin acted with haste in the waking hours when the voice wasn't present. His orgy of murder continued as he made his way south towards the yet unknown final destination. They were almost in a routine where Mad Martin would kill and mutilate, then receive a beating from Big Ed when he returned to possess him. The serial killer had worked out the voice needed his body. He didn't enjoy his punishments but figured they were worth it on balance for being able to have fun with his victims.

Big Ed was frustrated at not having total control over the serial killer. When choosing his host he had assumed the beatings would eventually weaken his mind, making him totally compliant. He was too near his target to find another host. Mad Martin had no intention of being caught and Big Ed acknowledged that he'd been reasonably careful in selecting the final resting place of most of his victims. If he had blood it would have boiled at the thought of one of the twins finding the first car and a body. He didn't have the time to deal with them now but the twins were added to his list. After Val joined him, he was determined they would be next to meet their maker. For now he needed to focus all his power on getting Val ready to accompany him. His host was on the outskirts of London and Big Ed felt strong and almost ready. He intended to pay Val one last visit before enlisting the help of Mad Martin to bring her to her final destination.

Chapter 19

It was obvious to the Director that Mad Martin had long since left Ailkirk. Having been officially stood down from the operation he was surprised when his PA buzzed to say the Minister was on the secure line. Although unprepared he had no choice but to take the call. He assessed the situation as he picked up the handset. He'd heard the PM had intimated the possibility of a cabinet reshuffle; so the Minister was obviously desperate for brownie points. The chances of him keeping his job were linked to the capture of Mad Martin so he must have decided to pull out all the stops.

'Thanks for your help so far, Director.'

'No problem, sir.' He decided not to take the bait and ask what he could do for the Minister.

They were both silent until the Minister realised he'd have to ask for assistance. This wasn't going as planned. 'We need all the help we can get to catch this bloody maniac.'

'Yes, sir. I understand that other regional forces have joined the hunt and all police leave, except compassionate, has been cancelled until he's caught.'

The Minister muttered something and the Director waited patiently for the question.

'Can your organisation help?'

'You know our charter, sir,' the Minister had approved the document. 'This is a criminal matter. The Chief of Police would be mortified if she thought you'd asked me for help behind her back.'

'Yes, yes, I know all that. But she doesn't have to know, does she?'

So he really was desperate.

'Perhaps we should all meet to discuss it, sir?' he decided to wind the bastard up for a bit. 'You never know, she might agree to hand over jurisdiction to a secret organisation with a small number of select employees. In fact, why don't you call in the SAS too and see what she has to say about that?'

The Minister coughed and the Director sighed. 'Please tell me you haven't, sir?'

'Look. Let's just stick to the matter in hand. Is there anything else you can do?'

The Minister was unaware the Director had his own ideas and was already onto it. 'Leave it with me, sir, I'll see what I can do.'

'What's your plan?'

'I think it's best that you don't know, Minister, then you won't have to lie if there's ever an enquiry.'

The Minister harrumphed and they hung up after the Director told him he'd be in touch, if and when there were any developments.

Recruitment was currently on hold so Violet and Fiona, along with a number of their Scottish based agents, had been working at the school helping the other staff to coordinate the operation. They had not yet returned to their normal duties.

'What time are Jim and Ryan due to arrive?' shouted the Director. Fiona told him that she'd had a text to say that they were in the lobby.

'Shall I send them in, sir?' he told his PA to do just that then motioned Violet and Fiona into the office.

Ryan and Jim arrived. They chatted while they made themselves comfortable around the table in the Director's office.

'How's Tony?'

'A lot better thanks. The doc reckons another week to be on the safe side. He's bored out of his brain and itching to get back to work.'

'Good news,' the Director nodded. 'Right. We've been asked to help the police, unofficially this time. Despite all the resources thrown into this operation Mad Martin is proving very elusive,' he bridged his fingers and frowned. 'There are suspicions that he's not working alone.' He explained that some of the bodies found had fitted his previous MO but others hadn't. 'The evidence thus far suggests he's making his way to an unknown destination down south. When he was in captivity he always said that he if he escaped he would go abroad at the earliest opportunity. So why hasn't he done that? Why stay here and increase his risk of recapture?' he nodded to Violet.

'All previous data shows he's a lone wolf, and always has been. We're all flummoxed so need to find a new way to discover his whereabouts and to stop him A.S.A.P.'

'That's where you and Tony come into it, Jim.' The Director took over and they all knew what was coming. 'Can you make contact with your sister to ask for help?'

*****

Libby felt deliciously naughty as she got out of bed at two o'clock in the afternoon. Tony reached over to slap her behind, a lascivious expression on his face.

'There's not much wrong with you, my love, is there?' she laughed. Two weeks earlier they'd made love for the first time since his accident and it had been tentative and a little awkward. They'd both been wary and concerned it might be too soon. This time he'd been his usual gung-ho self. As well as being on a high from the pure enjoyment of their lovemaking, Libby knew her husband had made a full physical recovery. He seemed to have got over the attack too but she'd read that it could stay with him forever so intended to watch out for any changes, just as the book advised. The phone interrupted her thoughts. Putting on her dressing gown she picked up the bedroom extension. Mouthing *it's your mother* to Tony, he watched as she nodded and frowned during the conversation. Eventually she handed the phone to him, despite him closing his eyes, feigning sleep, to avoid having a chat.

203

The call had swept away their early euphoria. Libby's concern was almost palpable, and he could feel her stress.

'Are you sure you're okay with this?' Her mother's condition seemed to be worsening and Libby had agreed to return to Marion's for a few days to offer help and support.

'Of course. I'm returning to work next week anyway, so it makes sense.'

'Your mother's seeing HER psychiatrist later.' Libby was still surprised at Marion's relationship so always emphasised he was her psychiatrist as well as her own mother's. 'She's going to ask him to Section my mother for her own good.' They were both stunned it had come to this. Marion really believed that Val would return to self-harming if they didn't act soon.

'I said I'd go tomorrow but do you mind if we go today? I don't really want her to be on her own for long while your Mum's out.'

Tony agreed. They each showered then started getting Libby's things together.

*****

Marion was glad to be out of the house for a while. Val was sleeping peacefully having taken a tablet to help. Libby had called to say she'd be there within an hour so Marion expected Val to still be sleeping by the time her daughter arrived. She'd left her on her own for short periods before so had no reason to believe this time would be any different. She let herself into the apartment that Basil had rented for their assignations. Although their relationship was now out in the open and were doing nothing wrong, she still felt like an errant teenager and giggled as she opened the door. Already in his dressing gown he pulled her into his arms then covered her in kisses, pulling off her coat and clothes as he kissed her. As well as adoring Basil, Marion was grateful to him. He'd reawakened her passion and proved a welcome escape from looking after Val. She questioned whether she'd still have her sanity if it hadn't been for him. They made love then napped for a while before talking about their plans for the future. Marion wasn't comfortable about discussing Val while lying naked with her lover, so they agreed not to let the situation spoil their afternoon. They always discussed Val prior to Marion's departure and today was no different. Dressed and drinking coffee while sharing a sandwich, Basil agreed to pay a house visit the following day to carry out another assessment. They said their goodbyes then Marion made her way home, totally oblivious to the chaos about to erupt.

*****

Gabriella was alert and appeared to be waiting for Claire. She wasn't surprised to see Raphael but was delighted all the same.

'I knew you'd return to us. How are you?'

She could see he wasn't too badly physically damaged but, like Claire, she wondered if the mental scars might take longer to heal.

Claire waited with as much patience as she could muster while they caught up with each other. When she deemed enough time had passed for her not to appear rude, she broached the subject of Val, firing questions at Gabriella like rounds from an automatic rifle.

Gabriella put her hands over her years. 'Tell me when she's stopped, Raphael.' It had the desired effect on Claire. She shut up and waited.

'The Committee told me it's her time, Claire, so it's out of my hands.'

'You mean she's used up all her heartbeats?'

'In a manner of speaking, yes. We haven't gained total control yet so don't know how it's going to happen.'

Claire was frustrated that not even Gabriella had all the answers. Her next thoughts were for Ron. 'What are you going to tell him?'

'I can't tell him anything. Val isn't old and appears to be in reasonable health without any signs of terminal illness. I can't say the same about her mental condition so we have to assume it's a sudden event. It's going to be traumatic for Ron whichever way he finds out, but I'd rather he wasn't exposed to prolonged trauma.'

Raphael and Claire agreed.

'I want us all to be there to support him when he needs us and we might have to help him to bring Val to us.'

The latter wasn't lost on Claire. So it was touch and go where Val would end up. This was going to be very distressing for Ron.

'Shall we?'

They went to find him, none of them looking forward to the task that lay ahead.

*****

Ron was delighted for Claire and over the moon that Raphael was back. They all settled down once the hellos were over, but Ron's antennae told him all was not well. He knew he had to guide someone's entrance to Cherussola but wondered why there was so much tension amongst his three angel companions. Surely Claire and Raphael should be more carefree, even if Gabriella wasn't. Slowly putting everything together, the truth hit him like a bolt of lightening. He stopped mid-journey, almost causing a collision.

'It's Val isn't it?'

'Yes, Ron. But we don't know when or how.' Gabriella repeated what she'd told the others with as much sensitivity as she could muster.

'So it could be a violent death or she could commit suicide. Nobody's knows yet?'

'It could also be an accident, Ron,' added Claire. 'She might fall down the stairs or something.' Claire doubted it but hated seeing his face contorted with pain.

'Can't you stop it, Gabriella? Change the weather or something? You've done that before. Or even ask the Committee to change their minds? Can't you do that?' He was panicking now but could see by their faces that this was a fait accompli. He took a few seconds in an attempt to dispel the panic. It was no comfort Val was coming to him at long last, so he tried to prepare himself for the gruesome task of viewing her death without being able to intervene.

Seeing Ron's reaction, the angels didn't want to burden him further. It would be too much for him to know that Val's future destination was touch and go. So although Ron thought he'd already heard the worst, from their perspective, ignorance was bliss. They carried on their journey but were pulled up yet again, this time by Claire.

'My brothers need to speak to me.' She explained Jim was trying to contact her and that it was urgent. 'He's saying something about a serial killer but I can't make sense of it.'

Gabriella was in a dilemma. She knew how much Ron needed Claire's support but she also knew the incredible pull Claire's brothers had on her. Gabriella had to be with Ron and would need plenty of assistance, especially if Val's death involved violence. None of them knew what to expect or how many evils might be involved.

'I'll come with you, Claire.' Raphael put a protective arm around her.

'No, you're needed here,' she touched his cheek and smiled. 'I'm stronger, Raphael. I'll be back as soon as I can.'

Gabriella was secretly proud of Claire. She'd long put behind her the dizzy blonde act and was now a team player, but was also capable of taking responsibility and acting alone. Her protégé was coming along nicely. Had they not been struck by disaster and swamped by evils Claire would still be a talented spirit. The chaos brought on by the overwhelming amount of evils had meant hasty promotion to angel, and Gabriella acknowledged that Claire deserved it more than anyone else she knew. She agreed she should go alone, but return as soon as she could. Raphael wasn't happy but knew it was the sensible option. He didn't want to upset Claire, irritate his sister or raise Ron's suspicions about why they needed so much strength to collect one human soul.

In Claire's absence Gabriella decided to call for assistance from Zach. He hadn't been fully tested since his rescue from Hell and neither had Raphael. She hoped that if the worse happened before Claire's return, they would be strong enough to deal with it.

*****

Claire was surprised to find Tony wasn't with Jim.

'Where's Tony? Is he all right?'

'He's made a good recovery and will be back to work next week. No long-term side effects.'

'Give him my love. I've been busy so haven't had a chance to visit, but obviously knew the worse didn't happen.'

'Will do.'

'Who's the grumpy looking bloke? He would be a catch for some lucky lady if he looked a bit happier.'

He laughed as he told her about Ryan, adding that he could be trusted.

Ryan watched, silently. Although Jim wasn't talking out loud his mannerisms told him he was having some sort of conversation.

'Anyway, Ryan knows about you but he's the one who was very sceptical to start with.'

'Was he now.'

Jim regretted his words as a number of newspapers on the desk fluttered to the floor.

'Is it her?' asked Ryan, folding his arms. He suddenly felt very cold. He watched in fascination as his jacket moved from the back of one chair and came to rest on the hook on the back of the door. Whilst he accepted Claire's presence, it was still disconcerting to witness her actions. White as a sheet and shaking, he stood up.

'I'm out of here.' He went to lift his jacket off the hook, shuddered, then changed his mind leaving the room without another word.

'A bit unnecessary, Claire.'

'Well, you said he could be trusted and I want to be absolutely sure he doesn't doubt you. If you're working together you don't want him thinking you're a nutter, now do you?' She knew it was an excuse to have a bit of fun and she should conserve her energy, but sometimes Claire just couldn't help herself. In addition, knowing what she was going to return to, it had eased her tension a little.

'Anyway, Claire. We need your help.'

While listening to her brother Claire scanned the horrific headlines whilst looking at the photographs in the newspapers she'd just scattered. Jim explained Mad Martin was still at large, assuming that Claire already knew of the sadistic serial killer. She was horrified when he elaborated on the nature of the crimes and was alarmed to hear Mad Martin most probably had an accomplice. It would have been difficult for her brother to understand she had other priorities and would add this one to her *to do* list. She agreed the safest place for Mad Martin was definitely behind bars, so told him she would do all she could to help.

'So who's his accomplice?'

'If we knew that, Claire, I wouldn't be asking for your help, but the so-called experts say it's unprecedented. He's always been a loner. They also expected him to leave the country at the earliest opportunity. It's almost as if something is driving him to a specific location...' Jim's words tailed off as he tried to get his head around the information.

'Like he's got another voice in his head or something?'

'Yes, Claire, exactly! The man's been examined by top psychologists, psychiatrists, you name it. The thing is though, there's no previous record of mental illness or other personalities showing, despite the, err, nature...yes, despite the nature of his crimes.'

Claire knew there was still much work to do to restore the equilibrium on Earth. Jim's comments now made her wonder if this devilish Mad Martin was possessed by one of the worst demons who they hadn't yet caught.

'Leave it with me and I'll get back to you.'

The Director would be happy with that. He breathed a sigh of relief. 'When, Claire?'

'It doesn't work like that, Jim. Have patience.'

He coughed to hide his chuckle. That was rich coming from his sister.

'I'll be in touch.'

There was no point in further questions. Jim knew she'd left.

As she made her way to re-join the others, Claire hoped Gabriella would make the capture of the serial killer her next priority after dealing with Val. She didn't even suspect the matter would resolve itself before she could raise the alarm.

Chapter 20

'Look, there's Libby.' Ron pointed to the scene below. Tony lifted Libby's case into the car before opening the passenger door for her. She giggled when he said *m'lady* and bowed as she entered the car.

'Isn't my brother a perfect gentleman?' They turned towards the voice as one and welcomed Claire back.

'What did he want?' asked Raphael. Gabriella told him to shush and watch the events unfolding below as the car pulled away from the pavement.

The scene changed to Marion's apartment. Val was lying in bed, breathing heavily. Ron assumed she wasn't dreaming as her face looked serene and unlined.

'She looks so peaceful,' he whispered, trying his best to keep his composure in view of what was to follow.

Outside they noticed a man walking toward the building. His hands were stuffed into his pockets and he was wearing a hood, despite it being broad daylight. The man must have looked mean to people walking the other way who crossed the road in order to avoid him. None of the angels could see his face as he neared. Instead of approaching the front door he gave it a quick look then carried on walking. At the end of the block he turned right and right again, heading down the lane toward the rear of Marion's apartment. Head still down he checked both directions. When no one was about he jumped over the fence and approached the back door.

'Oh no,' said Ron, watching in horror.

The man stopped mid-step halfway to the back door and shook his head. Suddenly he punched himself twice in the face and his head reeled backwards.

'What on Earth,' said Claire and her brother's words were starting to come back to her. They were all startled as the man changed his mind again. About six feet from the back door he took a run then jumped and kicked the door with his heavy boot. A split appeared in one of the panels and seeing the weakness he repeatedly kicked the same area.

'He doesn't seem bothered that he's making a lot of noise. Isn't he worried that he'll get caught?'

They all thought he looked like a man on a mission but nobody answered Ron as they continued to watch.

Now in the kitchen he was still as he listened for a moment. All was quiet so Val must have slept through the incursion. Still wearing his hood the man opened a drawer, selected a knife, then made his way upstairs.

He checked the bedrooms on the first floor. Becoming frustrated he quickly made his way up to the next. Putting the knife on the dressing table he approached the bed. She was dead to the world until the man tenderly moved a few strands of hair from her face then ran his fingers down a cheek. Coming slowly awake Val smiled at first. Her smile turned to a mask of fear as she opened her eyes and looked at the face smiling down at her. The man still wore his hood so Ron and the angels were unable to see his face. Even if they had, only Claire would have recognised him.

Val scurried over to the other side of the bed and rolled out of it onto the floor. The man couldn't reach her without moving but he didn't appear to be in any hurry.

Remembering he was still wearing his hood he threw his head back to remove it. He ruffled his hair with his hands and smiled at Val.

'At long last we're going to be together.'

Claire let out a screech and put a hand to her mouth. Raphael tried to comfort her but she pushed him away. 'That man's a serial killer. Jim wanted our help to find him!'

'Do something, Gabriella, please?' Ron pleaded.

Val didn't recognise the man in front of her for who he was. She hadn't seen the news or read a newspaper in some time and might have been the only person in the country who wasn't aware the notorious serial killer was on the loose. She wasn't any less frightened because whoever it was, she knew that Gary had taken over his mind and body.

'How could you do all those evil things and pretend to be a loving human being?' Val shuddered. She covered her mouth with her hand, biting her palm in terror. As he walked toward her she started slowly backing away.

'Come on, Val, Sandy deserved it. She didn't know how to treat me and she made me angry. I couldn't help myself. I never hurt you, darling, did I?' He didn't mention the young girls as he held out a hand for Val to take.

'I don't want to be with you, Gary,' she was whimpering now. 'It was a mistake and we didn't even sleep together.' Val was trying to convince herself as much as the intruder who took little notice of what she said as he moved slowly toward her, savouring each moment. He'd been waiting for so long for this and now picked up the knife from the dressing table, turning the handle around a few times to get a proper feel for the instrument. It was the first Val had seen of the knife and she gasped. She felt behind her in desperation. Touching the wall and the window she knew there was nowhere else to go.

In that instant Val knew that she was going to die. She also knew she didn't want to spend eternity with this man.

He made a small cut in his finger, watching in fascination as his own blood dripped slowly onto the floor.

Now that Val had accepted her fate she felt strong and determined for the first time in ages. She pushed open the window and climbed onto the outside ledge.

'I love Ron and when I die I'm going to be with him and nobody else.'

Gary bounded to the window following her onto the ledge.

'Gabriella!'

Claire held Ron's arm as they watched. He felt totally helpless and tried his best to look away, but like a rubbernecking motorist passing an accident he just couldn't help himself.

'I'm sorry, Ron but Val's going to die. Our intervention wouldn't stop that,' Gabriella wiped a stray tear from her cheek. 'There are two evils in her assailant's body, Ron. I know it's of little comfort to you but we're going to do our utmost to bring them to the cave today.'

For the first time Claire could actually feel Gabriella's pain and knew how much emotional effort the decision had taken. Zach put an arm around Gabriella and Claire noticed the expression on Raphael's face. So the wings communicated raw emotion as well. She learnt something new each day.

Sensing her intent Gary moved so he was directly in front of her. Val was now leaning into the window and Gary's back was facing nothing but fresh air. He needed both hands for balance and had to drop the knife. It clattered to the pavement where a small crowd had gathered. As Tony and Libby parked up down the road, they could hear police sirens in the distance.

'I wonder what's going on?' said Libby. Panic hit her insides when she saw the expression on her husband's face.

'That's my mother,' she shouted. The crowd parted as she ran to the pavement underneath the window.

'The police are coming, Mum. It's going to be all right. Leave her alone you bastard!'

Tony ran into the house and sprinted up the stairs. He entered the bedroom quietly, hoping to surprise both Val and Gary – but he was too late.

'I love you Libby... and I'm sorry.' Val called as Gary leaned forward to kiss her. She put her arms around his waist while opening her mouth to him. At the last moment she turned her head so his lips brushed her cheek. She smiled as she launched them both off the window ledge. *Ron* was the only word the onlookers heard before the concrete broke the two bodies. The last sound heard by Val was her own daughter's screams.

Already exhausted by his last efforts in Mad Martin's body, Big Ed wanted to use the little strength that remained to take Val to Hell. He was ill prepared for the ambush by the small host of angels. He used the last of his energy to summon evils to his aid but his calls went unanswered. Big Ed had nothing left. All he could do was watch in horror as Claire started transforming his human form to that of a cockroach.

The same couldn't be said for Mad Martin and it took the combined strength of Raphael and Zach to snare him.

'Jolly good show, old chap,' said Zach high-fiving Raphael after they'd caught him and placed him in the force field along with Big Ed.

As the angels were transforming the evils a darkness descended. Claire had transformed Big Ed up to his waist and her next efforts amounted to nothing. The darkness enfolded her and Big Ed like a malevolent cloak, and she could just make out the same happening to Raphael, Zach and their captive. Her last clear image of her beloved angel was of the effort on Raphael's face as he tried with his whole being to move toward her, to no avail. Gnarled hands appeared out of the darkness and Claire didn't understand how she could see the hands but couldn't see Raphael or Zach. The hands claimed Big Ed and Mad Martin and pulled them through the angel's force field as if it wasn't there. The hands disappeared but Claire was still able to see Big Ed and Mad Martin as they were transformed from human to animal then insect and back to human. This cycle repeated itself and they fought each other in their various guises. Each time their human form returned it was more broken and deformed. The torment showed clearly on their faces and they were exhausted, but still forced to perform by an invisible presence. Claire wondered how she could view this horror show when all else was in darkness. She watched mesmerised as the invisible presence tired of playing games, and both evil demons were suddenly naked, with broken limbs and faces bruised and deformed. Big Ed watched in horror as flames started to lick at the feet of Mad Martin. He screamed in agony as his skin melted and the slow flames flickered their way up his body. Mad Martin had stopped screaming by the time the fire reached his head. His eyes popped out of their sockets and a few seconds later nothing was left of the evil soul. Big Ed realised the finality of his situation.

'Master Of All Evil, My Lord. I'll do anything you say. Let me serve you...'

His grovelling came too late and Satan now showed himself. For an instant the image in front of Claire was of an evil red demon with horns and a tail. It changed into that of an old teacher, a man who had been jailed for interfering with children at her school. Yet again Satan changed his persona this time to a famous Rock Star who'd been convicted for his orgy of murder. Claire watched in morbid fascination as Satan displayed himself in the guise of the most evil people she could remember.

He threw a small fireball at Big Ed. Claire derived no pleasure from witnessing the agonising end of the evil man who'd caused so much grief to her own family and many others.

Satan turned to Claire and undressed her with his eyes. He leaned forward and she felt his hand on her shoulder. A desperate coldness hit her as if her whole being had turned to ice. She was pushed downwards. The hand had left but Claire was still travelling down and down. The ice cold turned to intense heat, searing her very soul.

'Oh no, no...' she whimpered. Claire closed her eyes, but much as she tried couldn't summon any loving memories. Then she heard the laughter, not a joyful happy sound, but an evil warning of the pain and sorrow to come. A voice in her head told her to open her eyes and she was powerless to resist. Satan blew on his index finger and it was aflame. He leaned forward and poked her. She could smell her skin sizzling and his imprint was now upon her. He laughed and licked his lips. *My new toy, you're coming with me* were the words in her head. Claire tried with all her might to close her eyes and Satan merely laughed.

'My Lord?'

From the depths of her despair Claire heard the squeaky posh voice call for help. She thought Zach's plea had come too late and lost all hope as she was pushed downward with the darkness.

'Take only your own and be gone.' Claire hadn't heard this voice before but knew exactly who owned it. Suddenly there was hope. Despite being in the possession of the master of all evil, Claire knew she wasn't going to Hell. She felt caressing warmth on her shoulder and watched in fascination as Satan's mark disappeared.

The first flash of light pierced the darkness followed by another and another then her world turned to bright light as Satan lifted a hand to cover his eyes. Claire looked up and the first image she saw was of an ancient man with long silver hair and beard. He was holding a staff and before she could get a good look, the image turned into that of her lovely grandmother.

'Nanna, nanna,' called Claire and the woman smiled at her before disappearing. This time the image changed into a kindly old gentleman who'd lived on Claire's street when she was young and had stepped in to help when bullies had chased her. All the good people she remembered from her life appeared before her until the image once again returned to its Godly form. Claire knew she was now safe and serenity replaced her earlier despair. She simply said *Thank you*. God smiled kindly. Claire wasn't surprised when an instant later the darkness disappeared and she felt herself enfolded in warmth that could only mean one thing. Opening her eyes again she squeezed Raphael as tightly as she could. Zach appeared at Claire's other side and she was relieved to see that neither had come to any harm.

A force field was weaved around the angels. They watched as God's smile vanished then he closed his eyes and lifted his arms, hands pointing towards Satan. Light came out of his fingers and the Master of Evil threw fireballs in return. The light hit the fireballs and exploded sending tremors throughout the atmosphere. Each bolt of light impacted with the fire moving nearer and nearer to Satan. He screamed in anger and frustration, knowing that if he remained he would be injured.

'Good will always prevail,' said The Lord as he threw one final powerful light. It hit the fireball before it left Satan's fingers and the Master of Evil screamed as he was invaded by love and compassion. The battle over but not the war, Satan transformed into a dark light and sped through the atmosphere back to Hell, intent on causing maximum pain and suffering on his arrival.

As God disappeared, so did the force field. The angels reflected on events and centred themselves, knowing it would be some time before the shock would wear off. There was still work to be done and they set off to find Gabriella and Ron, to see if they needed help with Val.

*****

Val was still in shock. Not only was she dead, but she had seen lights and heard explosions. She was still frightened even though all was now calm. As Ron welcomed her the anxiety disappeared as he explained they were going to be together forever. The beautiful angel asked Ron to be quiet and Val heard a whoosh. Another three angels appeared out of nowhere. She noticed they hugged and talked as if something awful had happened but all appeared uninjured except for some old scars on the two males.

'This is Claire, Val. She's your friend Marion's daughter.'

219

Val was overawed by it all. She was so glad to see Ron and hoped they'd have the chance to talk later. She also hoped with all her soul that he'd be able to forgive her. She didn't take in the fact that one of the beautiful angels was *The Claire*. All Val wanted was to be with Ron.

Gabriella had received instructions to go ahead with the original plan. Although the others had been shocked by their experience, she could see they hadn't come to any physical harm.

'This is where we split for a while. Raphael and Claire please go to the cave. You're required to do a duty there and will be recalled when your stint is over.'

Raphael resisted the urge to ask who had put his sister in charge and what her punishment involved. He wasn't looking forward to being a bat, but the time would pass quicker in the company of Claire; he was grateful for that at least.

'Zach. You're coming back to Cherussola with me. We've all done well and by the grace of God, the immediate danger is over. Things should start calming down on Earth and peace will reign for a while, but we must be ever vigilant. We came too close to disaster this time and can't afford to make the same mistakes again.'

'Ron. You have a choice but you will need to listen to what I tell Val before you decide.'

Just when Ron was starting to think all the drama was over, he realised there was more to come.

'Val, there's no easy way to say this. You've proved yourself to be weak, easily led and on occasion, deceitful. The Committee have hope for your soul but you still have many tests to pass. You will return to Earth and your next life will determine your final destination.'

'But...but, I thought I could be with Ron now. Don't you know how much I've suffered?'

'Yes. But the Committee knows you've brought on much of that suffering by your own actions.'

'The Committee? Who...'

'Val. Would you like to go to Hell now or have a second chance at life?'

Put that way it was a no brainer and Val remained silent as she tried to come to terms with her fate.

Ron had been watching and listening. More importantly he'd felt a release since Val's arrival he hadn't known since his death. It had taken a while for him to accept it but he reached the conclusion that what he'd felt for Val hadn't been the deep love he'd thought it was, but a sense of responsibility and duty. Now he no longer felt responsible for her, she had his sympathy. The longing had disappeared and there was only one soul he missed.

'Now your choice, Ron. Join Val or...'

'Can I go to the cave?' His true feelings had sneaked up on him but now he knew what they were, he wanted to be with her.

Val looked distraught but Ron knew the time had come to let her go and make a success or failure of her next life. On her own.

Gabriella beamed at him, knowing his friendship with Sandy went deeper but Ron had been blind to it, until now at least.

They said goodbye and went their separate ways.

Chapter 21

The Guano landed on the cockroach that Claire knew was Big Ed's father Harry, and she smiled with satisfaction. He looked up and saw the smiling bat, knowing instantly that these were the cave's guardians and not ordinary animals. This was confirmed when he saw a number of roaches try to leave and the bats dealt with them mercilessly.

The noise was so unbearable he didn't know if he could stand it. He'd had such hopes when joined by his son, now there was nothing.

'This screaming is driving me crazy,' he said, almost to himself.

'I've been mad for fucking years!' said the cockroach next to him. In the annals of his mind Harry recognised the line from an old song but couldn't quite place it. He had the rest of eternity to recall it and in total despair added his own voice to the screaming.

Acknowledgements

Thanks to my husband Allan for listening (or doing a good job of pretending to listen), to my fabulous editor Jill Turner and wonderful cover designer Jessica Bell. Thanks also to all my friends for their support.

Author's Note

Thank you for purchasing this book. I hope you enjoyed reading it as much as I did writing it.

If you like what you've read so far, you may be interested in my other books:

Beyond Possession (The Afterlife Series Book 4)
Beyond Limits (The Afterlife Series Book 5)
Beyond Sunnyfields (The Afterlife Series Book 6) coming soon

Unlikely Soldiers Book 1 (Civvy to Squaddie)
Unlikely Soldiers Book 2 (Secrets & Lies)
Unlikely Soldiers Book 3 (Friends & Revenge)
Unlikely Soldiers Book 4 (Murder & Mayhem)

The Island Dog Squad Book 1 (Sandy's Story) - FREE AT THIS LINK
https://dl.bookfunnel.com/wdh6nl8p08

The Island Dog Squad Book 2 (Another Crazy Mission)
The Island Dog Squad Book 3 (People Problems)

Court Out (A Netball Girls' Drama)

Non-fiction:

Zak, My Boy Wonder

And for children:

Reindeer Dreams
Jason the Penguin (He's Different)
Jason the Penguin (He Learns to Swim)

Further information is on my website https://debmcewansbooksandblogs.com or you can connect with me on Facebook:
https://www.facebook.com/DebMcEwansbooksandblogs/?ref=bookmarks

About the Author

Following a career of over thirty years in the British Army, I moved to Cyprus with my husband to become weather refugees.

I've written children's books about Jason the penguin and Barry the reindeer, and books for a more mature audience about dogs, the afterlife, soldiers and netball players, along with a non-fiction book about a very special boy named Zak.

'Court Out (A Netball Girls' Drama)' is a standalone novel. Using netball as an escape from her miserable home life, Marsha Lawson is desperate to keep the past buried and to forge a brighter future. But she's not the only one with secrets. When two players want revenge, a tsunami of emotions is released at a tournament, leaving destruction in its wake. As the wave starts spreading throughout the team, can Marsha and the others escape its deadly grasp, or will their emotional baggage pull them under, with devastating consequences for their families and team-mates?

The Afterlife series was inspired by ants. I was in the garden contemplating whether to squash an irritating ant or to let it live. I wondered whether anyone *up there* decides the same about us and thus the series was born. Book six is currently in the planning stage and I'm not yet sure when the series will end.

'The Island Dog Squad' is a series of novellas told from a dog's point of view. It was inspired by the rescue dog we adopted in 2018. The real Sandy is a sensitive soul, not quite like her fictional namesake, and the other characters are based on Sandy's real-life mates.

'Zak, My Boy Wonder', is a non-fiction book co-written with Zak's Mum, Joanne Lythgoe. I met Jo and her children when we moved to Cyprus in 2013. Jo shared her story over a drink one night and I was astounded, finding it hard to believe that a family could be treated with such cruelty, indifference and a complete lack of compassion and empathy. This sounded like a tale from Victorian times and not the twenty-first century. When I suggested she share her story, Jo said she was too busy looking after both children – especially Zak who still needed a number of surgeries – and didn't have the emotional or physical energy required to dig up the past. Almost fourteen years after Zak's birth, Jo felt ready to share this harrowing but inspirational tale of a woman and her family who refused to give up and were determined not to let the judgemental, nasty, small-minded people grind them down.

When I'm not writing I love spending time with Allan and our rescue dog Sandy. I also enjoy keeping fit and socialising, and will do anything to avoid housework.

Printed in Great Britain
by Amazon